MY BROTHER'S KEEPER

SHEILA KINDELLAN-SHEEHAN

MY BROTHER'S
KEEPER

A Toni Damiano Mystery

Véhicule Press

MONTRÉAL

Published with the generous assistance of the Canada Council for the Arts, the
Canada Book Fund of the Department of Canadian Heritage, and the
Société de développement des entreprises culturelles du Québec (SODEC).

Cover design: David Drummond
Typeset in Minion by Simon Garamond
Author photo by Dorothy Puga

Library and Archives Canada Cataloguing in Publication

Title: My brother's keeper : a Toni Damiano mystery /
Sheila Kindellan-Sheehan.
Names: Kindellan-Sheehan, Sheila, author.
Identifiers: Canadiana (print) 20230518419 | Canadiana (ebook)
20230518427 | ISBN 9781550656343
(softcover) | ISBN 9781550656428 (EPUB)
Subjects: LCGFT: Thrillers (Fiction) | LCGFT: Novels.
Classification: LCC PS8637.H44 M9 2023 | DDC C813/.6—dc23

Published by Véhicule Press, Montréal, Québec, Canada
www.vehiculepress.com

Distributed in Canada by LitDistCo
www.litdistco.ca

Distributed in the US by Independent Publishers Group
www.ipgbook.com

Printed in Canada on FSC certified paper

"Ceux qui s'en vont, ceux qui nous laissent,"
Those who go, those who leave us,
Mom
Michael
Thomas
And proclaim themselves in my veins.

If we are not our brother's keeper,
at least, let us not be his executioner.
—MARLON BRANDO

The past is never dead. It's not even past.
—WILLIAM FAULKNER

CHARACTERS

Major Crimes Team

LIEUTENANT DETECTIVE TONI DAMIANO confidently tackles a cold case that two investigative teams have failed to close. She learns that life is random.

DETECTIVE PIERRE MATTE, Damiano's long-time partner took the initiative and chose a cold case, trusting their skill and record. He also becomes Damiano's confidante.

CHIEF RICHARD DONAT, steely, demanding, has found that surviving a heart attack makes for a calmer perspective on work and a gentler chief of detectives.

The Rest of the Cast

THE TIBBETTS, STU AND CAROL. Unpopular in their neighborhood, but nevertheless, a typical suburban couple.

EMMA TIBBETT, daughter, divorced, working mother of three boys. She is also the victim of a dangerous hit-and-run.

CONNOR TIBBETT. Handsome, single, gay son, repudiated by his father, finds success as a financial advisor.

TIMOTHY LANG. Connor's partner whose love and support help guide Connor to the truth.

DEVON SHORE, Emma's ex, steps up to the plate when Emma is injured.

DOCTOR S. ZAGAN, oncologist. A meticulous surgeon concerned with patient care.

BARRETT, BRIAN AND MAGGIE. Young dentists living in Beaconsfield who lose thier two-year-old son in a terrible trangedy.

SANDRA HUGHES has begun a new career. Many years ago, she lost her husband to cancer and a smear campaign that cost him his job and hastened his death.

MARTIN HERON. A lonely, arrogant man who feels he could solve any mystery if it weren't for his panic attacks, paranoia, and red wine.

PAMELA GRANGER proves to Damiano that elders can be feisty, clever, compassionate, and fair in their assessment of others.

CHAPTER ONE

DETECTIVE PIERRE MATTE TOOK a minute to give his eyes a break. He'd spent four hours reading about a ten-year-old unsolved case and was deciding whether to ask for permission to take it on. With his palm, he rubbed the small window pane in the murder room then looked out to the heavy gray skies and stinging sleet! April was again proving Eliot right. Across the street he spotted a splash of purple in a tiny patch that must be a little garden fronting an old tenement building, grimy with age and soot from Crémazie Boulevard. It was his first sighting of a crocus pushing itself out of the mud. What was the line – *breeding lilacs out of the dead land, mixing memory and desire?* Too heavy for now, Matte thought.

His partner, Lieutenant Detective Toni Damiano was at St. Mary's Hospital following up on the mandatory yearly checkup. She'd been edgy yesterday and had chosen not to share her thoughts. Actually, he was happy for the peace. Damiano was loud, talkative and demanding. Intuitively, she was the better cop and his best friend. An odd couple to be sure – but together they were also the best duo in the Major Crimes department.

Matte had stacked the table with the previous investigations of the cold case which were conducted two years apart. Each file with photos, statements and notes made for such sizeable piles that he had divided them into four. After his readings, he followed his own style by reaching for photos of the couple before the incident. It was his work, and he hated the demeaning rummage through the lives of these victims, but he settled in. They were in their mid-sixties, both tall, carrying the weight of their years seemingly without denying themselves. The male, both actually, Matte thought, were the kind of neighbors that no one ever noticed. He was balding unkindly, had a round face with small eyes, a fleshy nose with reddish age spots, light stubble, and heavy jowls. He wore a checkered jacket and suit pants that didn't match. Something Matte would notice because Matte was always impeccably attired. He wore khakis with a blazingly white shirt with sleeves rolled to the elbows as though he had had help because both sides were so even. The band of his watch matched his pants. His brown hair was closely cropped.

The female had thick hair dyed blond and the stingiest smile he'd ever seen. It was easy to see who ran their show. Matte didn't bother with her clothes. Her face caught his attention. Determination had settled in on it, pinching the deep lines that cut from the sides of her cheeks down to her mouth. She was off balance, as though she had been pushed into the photo. Perhaps, Matte thought, he was being cruel. She might simply be unhappy, and she could join a multitude of women who felt the same.

The couple had two children, Emma and Connor, adults now. There was no mistaking their daughter Emma, a younger version of her mother, with an identical determined posture. Their son Connor was a surprise. He seemed to have the better genes of both parents. Tall and buffed, he wore a devilish smile, even in his thirties. Women and men, Matte knew, as a gay man himself, would have been attracted to him. The daughter was divorced with three children. The son was still single. Matte's radar was on alert.

He reached for the incident photos. A jolt of sadness as sudden as a stroke struck Matte as it always did when he studied victims of violence. This simple, ordinary couple didn't have the chance to live out their lives. The woman was slumped back on the sofa. Blood from her right temple ran down her face onto her neck and puddled on her green sweater. Her eyes were slits, and on her face, the leering grin of death. Her husband had crumpled onto her shoulder, shot through the right temple as well. The side of his face was bloody. His eyes appeared to register the shock of being cut down by surprise. The stippling of powder and debris on the temples of both victims indicated they were shot at close range. There was gun powder residue on the male's right thumb and index finger. The weapon was a common .22LR cartridge revolver. Neither victim had exit wounds, common with such weapons.

What first had appeared as a murder/suicide, sadly not uncommon, caused Matte to wonder why the husband was shocked – shocked that he had had the courage to go through with it, or shocked because they were both summarily executed. That was the question as Hamlet would say. Matte was met then, as the detectives before him had been, by the slow burn of the case. There was no weapon found at the scene. That was the choke – the reason the case was still unsolved.

Matte printed out his bullet points because he knew Damiano would speed read through the material and scribble notes that she herself would have trouble reading. The points: no evidence of forced entry – they admitted their killer because they knew him or they were duped; no evidence of an altercation; no defense wounds; no theft; all prints painstakingly recovered were unremarkable; no gun, no shell casings.

Cui bono? There were no millions. At the time of his death, Stu Tibbett was still teaching at a private school on the West Island and his wife Carol, three years younger, was a special needs school teacher in Verdun, quite a distance to travel every day. After seven years, the insurance company, with some reluctance and added stipulations, paid the policies. The son and daughter finally each received $300,000. They sold the house for $450,000; their parents' savings amounted to a little less than $200,000. The $1,250,000 was nothing to sneeze at. If indeed it was a murder/suicide, there was reason for the son, who discovered the bodies, to get rid of the gun, if not for his parents' reputation, then for the insurance money, non-applicable in the case of suicide.

This tragedy was either a murder/suicide or a premeditated cold-blooded murder, committed by their children, or someone who hated them enough to want them dead.

Matte knew where he wanted to begin. He reached into the pile of photos on his desk and pulled out the one of their home, a lovely property by Lac St-Louis on Manresa Court in the affluent area of Beaconsfield below Lakeshore Road. How could a couple of such moderate means afford the place? Inheritance, perhaps. Matte intended to find out. Neither file had mentioned this point. Matte grabbed his blue blazer and headed out to the West Island. Depending on traffic, a thirty-minute drive. Real estate interested Matte. One's home revealed a good deal about its owner. He parked on the court and had rung the doorbells of four homes before he found what he needed. Three owners who were home remembered the sad tragedy, but only the last was around when the home was bought by the Tibbetts.

She was a sprightly woman, probably in her seventies, with a warm smile that didn't extend to an invitation inside out of the rain.

"I'm alone and my son has definite rules as long as I'm determined to stay out of the clutches of retirement homes. The porch is a decent shelter. Wait here till I fetch my coat." She took a couple of steps. "Show me your badge." Matte complied, smiling. "I changed his diapers. Oh, rules be damned. Come inside. I find the kitchen much cozier if you don't mind. Don't bother taking off your shoes. I can mop up later. It's only water." Matte kept his blazer on to maintain the official nature of the visit. "This is exciting, Detective! What can I help you with?"

Matte liked her right off. She still had dimples. She moved quickly but she offered no coffee. He would have enjoyed a good cup.

"In cozy English mysteries, every old woman sets a table. I say let's get down to the business at hand. Since my Art died, I do what I want, within Michael's rules, when he's around that is. You don't seem the type to waste time with fluff talk, Detective Matte."

"You're right on that point, Ma'am. The Tibbetts bought their house twenty years ago. The asking price was $350,000. I was flummoxed as to how they considered the purchase on teacher's salaries. By the way, I don't have your name."

"Pamela, Pamela Granger. I know the story behind the story – it's so very sad. The young Barretts who owned the house, Brian and Maggie, were both dentists. Maggie had decided to take a two-year leave of absence to care for Calvin, their little son. Both were aware that Lac St-Louis was a stone's throw from their solarium. Calvin was a beautiful, innocent child. He wasn't a rascal – he was a runner. One forgets how quickly children move. He was just two with silky blond hair that had never been cut. He was cuter than a Gerber baby. Maggie left him in the locked solarium with his toys and ran to the kitchen to grab the doctor's phone. As you can see, we lived beside them. I heard Maggie's desperate scream. I'll never forget it. I ran out to join her. Calvin had managed to unlock the solarium door and was not in the house. We ran down to the river and found him immediately. His little body was swirling and bumping into a rock close to the shore. The water wasn't even two feet deep there. Maggie jumped in and pulled him out, laid him on the ground and attempted CPR. I ran to the house and called for an ambulance. The toddler was gone. He must have fallen into the river. The rocks are dangerously slippery. She refused to let go of her baby. Maggie was lying alone on the ground, keening with Calvin in her arms. She looked no older than a child herself. The first responders kindly gave her time because the boy was beyond help.

"In these awful tragedies blame is thrown around and eats away at the marriages. We tried to help, their own parents tried too, but before we knew it, they put the house on the market. The loss of Calvin broke them. Maggie just wanted to get out. They sold the house a few months after Calvin drowned in 2002.

"The Tibbetts' son knew the real estate agent and he advised them to make a lowball offer. The house was listed at $350,000. They offered $200,000, and Maggie and Brian accepted. Brian was reluctant, but Maggie's parents had helped them with the purchase. The home was listed in both their names, but Maggie held sway. She wanted out. Calvin was in every room, and she couldn't breathe. The Tibbetts boasted of the steal they had made and became pariahs to all the neighbors. Who would boast of taking advantage of such a tragedy? I was aghast and I wasn't alone.

"Before you go, Detective, there is something else. If the Tibbetts were murdered, I want to help. I'm no gossip – people aren't that interesting. The Tibbetts never seemed to be comfortable here, and I think they were purposely unfriendly. They threatened to take the couple across the street to Small Claims Court because their dog relieved himself on their lawn despite the fact that the Brits scooped and spritzed. The Tibbetts were not pleasant people."

"You've been a real help, Mrs. Granger. Thank you."

"Pam, please. Before you leave, despite how they conducted themselves, I feel sadness for the Tibbetts. They reminded me of the school kids who spent their young lives looking in from outside, and that didn't change for the Tibbetts."

Matte understood only too well, though 'aghast' was still the right word. The Barretts became new suspects in the investigation. They had not been mentioned in the two previous ones.

CHAPTER TWO

LIEUTENANT DETECTIVE Toni Damiano sat outside the CT scan room checking her watch. There were four other patients sitting outside in the corridor waiting for Godot as well. She had figured she'd be in her car by now, driving back to the division on Crémazie Boulevard. Her scan was done, she expected nothing untoward. She was already put out that Matte was studying their prospective case without her. She was back at St. Mary's Hospital in the borough of Côte-des-Neiges and Notre-Dame-de-Grace where forty-four years ago she'd been born. A homecoming of sorts, she thought.

She straightened the pin-striped jacket of her tailored black suit, noticed a few glances coming her way and ignored them. Why was she still waiting? Surely nothing had gone wrong with the scan. They'd already assured her that she did not have pneumonia as had been indicated with the first X-ray. She shifted her body on the plastic chair. When her phone rang, she thought it was Matte.

"Toni, this is Doctor Zagan. I've pulled a favor, and my colleague, Doctor Jolie, at the Montreal General will see you later today. Doctor Jolie's patient load is heavy, so get to the hospital as soon as possible. Please be patient, Detective. We are all busy people."

"I don't have pneumonia, Doctor. I'm healthy."

"I've already spoken with Jolie. He'll be with you as soon as he can."

"But…"

"Toni, please."

"Fine, but you've seen my blood work. I'm healthy as a horse."

"Call me back after you've seen Jolie."

Damiano didn't feel a poke of fear. In her view it was all a waste of time, her time. Damiano followed Zagan's instructions. After more than two hours in the crowded waitng room, a slim, tall doctor in a white coat adjusted his glasses, looked at the waiting patients and approached her.

"Lieutenant Damiano, would you please follow me."

It was his gentle demeanor and the soft voice that caught Damiano off-guard and she followed the physician as if she was a child following the school principal. Once inside the sparse office, the only files were the ones Jolie carried, and she fended off what was coming before he had the chance to speak.

"Doctor there is nothing wrong with my lungs. I had pleurisy when I was a child. The day before I was to start work on the force, a doctor called me at home in the evening. I'd had the usual chest X-ray. I was twenty-two back then. He went on to tell me that I had tested positive for TB. He asked me if I was coughing up blood? I was young and sure of myself. I fought back, but stammered. 'I don't even have a cold!'

He didn't bother with my reply. Patients often lied to him, he said. I told him I didn't lie, and I had to begin work the next day. He became more forceful. Before any work, I was to repeat the X-ray. I shouted into the phone that what he was doing to me was unfair. I recall vividly what he said. 'It's fair to the general population if, in fact, you do have TB. Surely, you understand the implications.' I met him at the Lachine General. Two days later, I was declared healthy. I almost lost my job and four pounds."

After her story, Damiano said with confidence, "Doctor Jolie, so you see, I know about faulty diagnoses due to the damn pleurisy."

"Unfortunately, there were few CT scans back then. What I see from your scan today is scarring from the pleurisy, or a possible carcinoma."

Damiano went silent.

"As a favor to Doctor Zagan, I've arranged for you to have a PET-scan, here at the hospital, two-and-a-half weeks from today." He handed Damiano the appointment card. "I'm sorry, but I feel if it is cancer, we catch it early, and you live out your life." He got up and left, fading like a ghost.

Damiano tried her best to appear pleased, but her nerves got the better of her. When she caught her breath, she rushed unsteadily out to her car and called Zagan. "I'm not going through with this bogus diagnosis. I run, I'm never out of breath. I saw my best friend, a smoker, die of lung cancer. There's the agony, the pain, the chemo, the wasting away and the fear, always the fear. She told me she didn't even recognize herself. Even if you manage to survive, you're always afraid. That's not for me. There is no cancer in our family."

"Toni, Doctor Jolie and I spoke before he saw you. I don't know what it is, but he assured me it was not a type of familial cancer. I want you, for your own good, to make an informed decision."

"Why now?"

"Why not now?"

"Shit!"

"Agreed. I want you to bring someone with you when I receive the results of the PET scan."

"You just made it worse. You're leaning toward cancer."

"It wasn't my intention."

"I have to go."

"Take the scan."

Damiano punched the steering wheel until the palm of her hand was bruised. No one could help her. Words of comfort meant nothing, changed nothing. She felt completely alone. When had she lost her friends? Her badge was her life. One by one, she had abandoned them. What had she done with her life when it came down to it? As a wife, she was a 'C' at best. As a mother, she was a 'truant'. In books she'd often read the universal lament: 'There just wasn't enough time.' Those words never meant much until today. What if she didn't have the time to improve? She'd meant to, but there was never enough time. Damiano grunted morosely. At this stage of her life, Damiano thought she'd be a better person, not just the cop that everything had come easily to as Matte had said. She wasn't going to confide in her husband Jeff or her son Luke because they'd side with Jolie. Matte was the only person who might understand because he'd faced fear all his life.

CHAPTER THREE

DAMIANO HAD THOUGHT of stopping off for coffee before heading back to the division, but her nerves were so tight they hurt, and her shoulders were whiplashed and refused to relax. Caffeine was the last thing she needed. When she reached the sixth floor, she urgently scanned the newly-installed cubicles, looking for Matte. *Damn!* She remembered he was studying a new case and hurried to the murder room. She found Matte surrounded by files and photos, pinching the bridge of his nose with his eyes closed in thought. He didn't hear her enter.

"How's the case going?"

"Still looking for our hook. Complex is the first word that comes to mind." Matte looked up. "Everything go alright?" When there was no response, he gave Damiano his full attention. "What happened, Toni? Did you fall or something?"

"Pierre, can I trust you?"

"You need to ask?"

"This can't get out!"

"Sit down before you collapse and take as long as you need."

Detail by detail, she did just that.

"Do you want my input?"

"I'm not taking the PET scan. That's where they send cancer patients. I don't have cancer. Even if I do, I never wanted to live forever. Chemo devastates the body. I refuse to be frightened like I was when they told me I had TB. I run and I have no shortness of breath. I've seen no changes. I'm healthy. Doctors don't take into account that patients know their own bodies. My friend who eventually died told me she regretted the chemo and experimental trials. She should have lived out her life. All that nausea and pain destroyed what life she had left and to quote her, 'It didn't change a freakin' thing. I was dying. Do you know that the survival rate of small cell lung cancer is about five percent? I never had a chance. I wish I had made my own choices.' Well, that's not going to be me."

"Get over here." Damiano folded into his arms. And he felt her relax. Damiano was reluctant to break apart. Shyness, but only for a moment. She couldn't recall if they had ever shaken hands. "Gays give the best hugs."

"You do, Pierre. I don't know about other gays. I also know you think I'm spoiled and immature – I could go on."

"That's not all true. What I respect and admire most is you chose me to be your partner, and my sexual preference never entered into that choice."

"That's because I saw your meticulous printing. Anyone with that precision and clarity would make a good cop. The devil is in the details, and God knows you pay attention to detail. Every cop, but you, has to work on that essential of the job."

"Do you want the truth?"

"Yes."

"I agree with you that you probably don't have lung cancer. Do you realize how many surgeries have been delayed, how many other needy patients can't even get an appointment due to the pandemic? Your MD called in a favor, and this oncologist took time out of his busy day to confer with you. Maybe that's because you're a public servant. Whatever the reason, people reached out to help you."

"I didn't ask either of them for help."

"Grow up, Toni!"

"An informed decision, that's the way Doctor Zagan phrased it."

"Well, you have two weeks to decide – don't be rash, Toni. Use the time."

"Two weeks of stress. Shit, Pierre I'm…?"

"That's normal. Look I have two days owed to me. I'll go with you if you decide to go. No one has to know, not even Jeff. By the way, this is a difficult case I have here."

"Let's go for it. I need to be engrossed in something other than the scan and my lungs. I'll stay late tonight and read. Leave your notes. I want to know the principals before we approach the chief."

"Take the files home. It's uncomfortable here."

"I don't trust myself to go home early."

"Understood. There's a salmon sandwich, and celery in the fridge. I was so caught up reading that all I ate was my apple."

"Ever dependable. Thanks. All I've had was a bagel that should have been tossed. I'll call home to cover myself."

"Tomorrow then."

"I'll be here."

For the next six hours, Damiano read, forgetting the sandwich, warding off the words *not a familial cancer.* Her back ached, her eyes watered from time to time, but she read on, captivated. "This is not a ten-year-old crime. It began twenty years ago when the Tibbetts literally stole $150,000 from the Barretts because they were so numb with grief that they were helpless to protect their assets. We start with Brian Barrett. I hope he's still in Quebec. He was never interviewed."

CHAPTER FOUR

THE OATMEAL HAD ALREADY come to a slow boil before Jeff made an appearance in the kitchen. Damiano was filling a yellow bowl and adding sliced banana coins and raspberries.

"That's what a late night will do to you, Toni. By the time your head hit the pillow you were dead to the world, so I didn't have the heart to ask how the medical went yesterday." He brushed her cheek with a kiss while reaching for his own bowl.

"I'm healthy as a horse, but there were the usual delays."

"You might have called."

"I'd already missed more than half a day's work and I wanted to catch up on a new case we're looking at. Do you recall that murder/suicide in the West Island years ago that made all the papers and media but was never closed?"

"As a matter of fact, I do. The police were missing something, right?"

"A weapon."

"Yes, that would clog things up."

"It has. Pierre and I want to close it if we can."

"For late nights, at least call. I was worried."

"Yes, Mother. Kidding, you're right."

"I'm off too, busy day."

"Luke?"

"Late day courses."

"Too old for a kiss."

"Enter at your own peril."

Damiano dashed up the stairs, opened Luke's door softly, approached the mangled covers, found a cheek, kissed it and tip-toed out.

Luke smiled, but didn't move.

Five minutes later, she was driving down Summit Circle on her way to Crémazie Boulevard. Damiano looked rested, but her navy slacks, pale blue cashmere sweater, gold accessories, and free-flowing curly dark brown hair couldn't hide the inner tension Matte could see. "Well, let's give this a try, Pierre. We are certainly not lacking for suspects. The reason for the murder or murder/suicide might not have occurred on the day of the crime, agreed?"

"Yes."

"We start with Brian Barrett."

"Let's go to Chief Donat first. We need his approval."

"Lead on."

Denise Roy, Chief Donat's secretary, would have been the perfect prison warden. There were no niceties, and she didn't mellow with age. She'd shrunk in size and hardened in her dealings with the officers who came to her office. What didn't change were her comfortable shoes and dresses from the nineties that were her uniform. "What exactly do you want?"

"I think we'll save that for the Chief."

"*I* inform the chief."

"I'm afraid I've caught you on that one, Ms. Roy. Our business is private."

Ms. Roy scowled. "Wait here."

"We won't move a muscle."

"Give her a break, Toni."

"Why?"

"Her job is all she has."

Before Damiano could respond, Roy appeared. "You may see the chief."

"Thank you," Damiano said too sweetly.

Chief Donat didn't stand as usual, but remained seated on his elevated leather chair. He listened as both Damiano and Matte introduced the unsolved case, then informed them he already knew about it.

"In Toronto, the case of the prominent couple found hanged about four years ago is still not solved, even with private intervention and the best teams on the case. Ours is a very ordinary couple from the 'burbs. What chance do you have where others have failed?"

"We might well fail, Chief, but we did find the remains of that child last year. These people are ordinary in every way. At the very least, one of them was murdered, without resistance, and we want to know why. We have enough photos and documentation to cover the murder wall. We just need your permission to get started. Before you decide Chief, Alfie, the couple's Airedale, was surrendered to the SPCA. Odd, don't you think? Not one of the children wanted it."

"Maybe. Look, I have to impose a deadline – how about two weeks? I can't have my best team wasting valuable time on an unsolvable case."

"That's fair. We're ready to begin. Thanks, Chief."

CHAPTER FIVE

"You're very wired, Toni. You really up for the work?"

"I need it, or I'd – I'd fall apart. Waiting is the worst."

"Donat doesn't want anyone pasting photos on the wall because we remove the paint when we take them down."

"We need two other corkboards then."

"I'll borrow them from Domestic. They have five."

"While you're there, I'm going to try and locate Brian Barrett. He'd be around fifty-four and certified in Quebec, so we should be able to locate him unless the family has left the province." Damiano was checking her iPhone as she spoke. She Googled them first. "Well, that was easy." She found a "Brian Barrett, dentist" located at 1 Holiday Avenue, Pointe Claire. "That's a business address. I know the place, three gold buildings." Damiano made the call and identified herself.

The receptionist briefly hesitated. Damiano learned that both Barretts practiced there. Brian was with a patient, but his wife had just finished with her patient. Damiano thought quickly. The odds were heavily weighted that they'd located the right couple. Even after twenty years, she didn't want to unduly upset the wife. They needed all the information they could manage, and the husband seemed a better bet. "How long will Doctor Barrett be?"

Damiano heard the receptionist checking the file. "Roughly, without incident…oh, here he is. We call Doctor Barrett the Roadrunner, he's so fast and accurate. Doctor, you have a call."

"Can't you take a message?"

"It seems serious, Doctor., it's the police" Barrett grabbed the phone. "Yes?"

"Doctor Barrett, this is Lieutenant Detective Damiano of Major Crimes."

"Lori, transfer the call to my office." Barrett didn't rush to his office because he was scouring his mind trying to figure out the reason for the call. "We have some peace now. What is this about?"

"My partner and I would like to meet with you. We've read the file and we know it was a tragic time in your life. We are reopening the Tibbetts' case, and we hope you might be of some help. We'd be very grateful for your assistance under the circumstances. In particular, we'd like to begin with the sale of your house."

Barrett didn't speak. Damiano gave him time. "It's been exactly twenty years and four days since we lost Calvin – it still seems like yesterday. I was never interviewed. I'm willing now, but I don't want my wife involved in any way. We didn't simply lose the house; I almost lost my wife and our marriage. Ask anyone who has lost a child if they are ever the same. I'd like the interview over as quickly as possible. My wife has yoga tonight. You'd be helping me out if we could meet here. I don't want her getting wind of this interview. Maggie has never forgiven herself, and the ground under her is still unsteady."

"Can you make yourself available in the next hour?"

"Yes. I'll reschedule. Call me on my private line, and I'll make certain Maggie has left for yoga. I'll be waiting at the front door of the clinic, second floor, Suite 207. It's the main building. As you enter, turn right for the elevator."

"We'll be there."

Matte had stood quietly by the door while Damiano was on the phone. "Where are we going to be?"

"We're meeting Brian Barrett at that gold-colored building behind the Holiday Inn in Pointe Claire in one hour. We go to the main building, the middle one. It's the quickest and best I could do."

Damiano drove the unmarked car, so they were in Pointe Claire ten minutes early. "I'll take notes, Toni, as usual."

From Damiano's point of view, Barrett didn't look his age. He wore a tight-fitting white cotton Polo shirt with the half collar that was popular on the tennis courts, and black pants. His mask was white and his hands were still gloved. Like Matte, he was slim rather than buffed. His eyes were the kind that commanded yours.

"Follow me."

Barrett joined Damiano and Matte discreetly and led them to his office without arousing the suspicion of his receptionist. His office was small, probably used for prep explanations to nervous patients.

"How about I begin and fill you in on the back story?"

"Fine," Damiano agreed.

"You've read about the loss of Calvin. We're both devastated. Our hearts died with Calvin. Maggie was severed in two, racked with guilt, which I made worse, lost to anything else, like the house. As his only child and for her protection, her father bought the house outright before our wedding. The house, though in our names, was hers. My parents didn't have the same resources, but they helped us out with the dental equipment. I took care of the funeral arrangements, but like Maggie, I was in the grip of loss and pain. There was never even a For Sale sign on the lawn; the real estate agent must have had inside connections. Most nights back then, I stayed out drinking at McKibbin's Pub cursing Maggie. All she had to do was watch Calvin! I never knew she'd sold the house until it was too late. We couldn't talk to one another for days.

"What snake robs a helpless woman and boasts to neighbors! If not for Calvin, I would have gone after them. But everything was moving so fast. Like I said, I was in a fog: selecting a casket for a two-year-old, picking out his favorite clothes, making arrangements with the priest at St. Edmunds. I hadn't been to church since Calvin's christening. What kind of God stands by and does nothing while a little boy whose only faults were innocence and the ability to unlock doors he couldn't even reach, drowns? Maggie sat beside me at the funeral, but we weren't talking. Two days later, she went back to her parents. I packed up the furnishings, stored some, and brought the rest to an apartment at Southwest One in Pointe Claire on Seigniory Avenue, and started working long hours. For two weeks Maggie never called. I was mired in anger and denial and couldn't forgive her. My parents talked to me about forgiveness, but I wouldn't hear of it. I'd lost my son!

"A few months later, Maggie finally called, at two in the morning, weeping. At first, I couldn't make out what she was saying. 'I'm pregnant, Brian.' That had been our plan, to have the children early, so we could work in the practice together. I grabbed some clothes, blew red lights till I reached their Westmount home. I found Maggie sitting alone on the top step. I took her in my arms, and we held one another until the shaking stopped. Maggie moved back with me to the one-bedroom apartment. I wasn't aware of time. We were together and we were safe, and I worked late, six nights a week.

"Nine months later, we had a baby girl with Maggie's dark green eyes. When I was burping Piper, she wouldn't lay her head on my shoulder, she preferred snuggling into my neck. She hooked me early. There is something about daughters that steal your heart. Two years passed, and I don't think either one of us saw them. I do recall the day Maggie had to pick dry-cleaning up and left Piper with me. She was playing with colored blocks and dolls. I grabbed the *Gazette* and was reading the editorial page about the supposed lack of French in the city. *What rubbish!* More people in Montreal speak French than ever before. A wary silence made the hairs on my neck rise. I ran through the house screaming, calling for Piper. She was gone. A sheen of sweat covered my body. *I've lost my daughter!*

"I ran out the side door I found open. My heart throbbed, I looked in the yard, I ran out front. She was nowhere. I shouted her name as I ran. Sweat dripped from my forehead. I screamed and turned up the block. And there was my little girl, casually following the garbage truck. I ran and scooped her up in my arms. She squirmed because I was holding her too tightly. It had taken me two years to understand. I waited for Maggie, waited to tell her I finally understood Calvin's death was an accident. It was an accident. We've never forgotten Calvin, and always celebrate his birthday. We made certain Piper knows her brother's photo and we've told her about him. 'He's an angel, right Dad?' I tell her Calvin's her guardian angel."

"Doctor, you own a .22 revolver. I read the registry."

Damiano wondered where Matte had found the time.

"I do. My father was an American, and it was his. I keep it in the safe at home. I didn't kill the bastards, but I was glad they were dead."

"Have you discharged the gun?"

"Once at a firing range. It's not the weapon."

"We'll follow you home and pick it up for verification. Your address?"

CHAPTER SIX

BACK IN THEIR CAR as they waited on Doctor Barrett to close up, Damiano said, "If Barrett has dual citizenship, how difficult would it have been for him to purchase another .22 and smuggle it across the border?"

"Would he have taken the risk of losing his wife and daughter, as well as his career, when their lives were thriving? Understood that they'd never recover from the loss of their son."

"Pierre, what if he thought he could commit the murders and walk away? Two teams of detectives never even interviewed him. Dentists have to be neat. The murders were executed with precision. The initial thoughts of murder suggested a professional hit, if indeed it was murder."

"Here he comes. He's two minutes from home. When his daughter Piper graduates, Barrett said he said he'll rent an apartment in the city for her, and they will move to the Southwest One penthouse. Nice plan." They drove in silence for the few blocks to Seigniory. "Parking will be fun."

"None of your shenanigans. We park when we find a spot." That was around the long corner. They walked back to the building. Matte checked his phone and buzzed 1046. The front door buzzed them inside and they waited and waited for an elevator. Once inside and on their way to the tenth floor, Matte looked closely at Damiano. "Not again!"

"Airplane bottle, just a swig. I was offered meds and I refused."

"So, you're self-medicating."

She took the bottle from her side pocket and showed Matte. "Not even an ounce."

"I won't work with you if you start up again." When they reached the tenth floor, Damiano threw the bottle down the refuse chute.

Barrett's door was opening, so Matte dropped the subject, but he knew Damiano's ruses. In nine-and-a-half years you learn a lot about your partner. "We have a few more questions, Doctor Barrett. The incident occurred on May eleventh, a Thursday night, between seven and ten." As Matte took the plastic box from Barrett containing his father's gun, he asked casually. "Do you by any chance remember where you were?"

"Before I answer your question, I'm repeating, you're wasting your time. That's not the gun."

"I like to be certain, Doctor. Now, to my question."

"Do you recall where you were ten years ago, Detective? As a matter of fact, up until four years ago, Thursdays I worked late, still building up the practice and purchasing a new home. I finished at eight and returned home to sushi and a glass of good wine. We'd moved to Brock Avenue in Pointe Claire by then."

Matte paused purposely to allow Barrett to fully comprehend where he was headed. The living room drew his attention, large, rectangular and richly appointed. The patio doors offered a good view of the pool enclosed by tall, trimmed white spruce. On one side of the room a soft, puffy caramel sofa sat across from a black and gray lined sofa with a single heavy leaden table between, all obviously custommade, perhaps Avenue Design. The wall that he faced was panelled wood with a golden tinge, and the whole room was dominated by one piece of art. He walked over and read its title 'Beauty in the Fleeting Moments'. He turned to Barrett, "Is it a genuine piece?"

"Yes, it was my father-in-law's gift to the family when Piper graduated. To this day I have never checked its value, but it's alarmed and insured."

Without another word, Matte asked quietly, "Your wife can alibi you then?"

"Actually no, she and Piper usually went to some play, mostly at the Centaur downtown. Do I need an alibi?"

"It would certainly help. You have motive and opportunity and perhaps a weapon."

"I wouldn't risk my freedom on those two. I'll call Jean Lefebvre, my lawyer. I suppose I've been too forthcoming already. I'll just add, much as I loathed what they were, they were not responsible for Calvin's death, but they added to our grief. Had they been responsible, I'd have shot them both. I think you'd better leave."

Damiano clenched her fists by her side, but kept silent until Matte and she were back in the car. "Don't ever grab a case from me without my consent."

"I did it for your own good. What if Barrett had smelled alcohol on your breath? You'd be suspended or worse. We are all getting too old for such behavior."

"You have no idea how scared I am. What if I have lung cancer? When I said I never wanted to live forever, I didn't mean dying in a year. I thought you'd understand how stressed I am, Pierre."

"Fear! I live with fear every day, Toni. Walking alone down a street at night I've been chased, beaten, spat on and kicked in the head because I'm gay. For starters, add loneliness until I met Matthew. I had no one to talk to, my father was ashamed of me, my mother loved me, but not when he was around. All cops have problems. It's the job. Until now, you've been lucky. Don't talk to me about stress."

She found herself shrieking, "If I confided in Jeff, he'd take my temp every day, run blood work twice a week and give me lectures on health, his forte. His love would smother me and fuel the fear because he'd outline the next procedures. I'd be living with cancer every day and not losing myself in a cold-blooded murder."

They laughed nervously. "I have some Ativan," Pierre revealed.

"Really?" Damiano's face lit up.

"No alcohol, Toni."

"I'll try."

"You can't just try. You *can't* drink, Toni! We'll leave Barrett to stew for a while and then summon him in for a formal statement. I'll do some checking on a second gun."

"What about Maggie Barrett? Those least suspected, like the butler?"

"I haven't forgotten her, Toni. I say we start with the Tibbett children."

"Alright."

"Are *you* okay?"

"Did you bring the Ativan?"

"Are you still alert for the case?"

"Alert as I can be. Fear is debilitating."

"You have to work through it. Why don't I give you the Ativan at the end of the day?"

"I'll need it. You can't forget!"

"I know and I won't."

CHAPTER SEVEN

"WHILE WE'RE DRIVING back to the division, do you have Connor Tibbett's number on your phone?"

"Do you have to ask?" Matte was already tapping in the number. It took a few seconds. "Whadda ya want?"

"Detective Pierre Matte, here. Am I speaking to Connor Tibbett?"

"Sorry, I thought you were someone else."

"Mr. Tibbett, we are reopening your parents' case."

"I wish you'd let them rest in peace, and Emma and me as well. I've answered the same questions so many times! The questioning brings that horrible night back. I have no faith you'll ever close the case."

"We are working for them sir, not necessarily for you. We would like to meet with you tonight."

"Sorry, I have plans."

"You also had parents. Don't they deserve your help? You were also first on the scene. You might recall some detail, something you didn't think important at the time, something."

"Same place? The Crémazie Division?"

"How about seven, gives us all time to grab a bite."

"I do want to help, Detective – sorry I came off as bloody selfish."

"We'll meet you at the main door."

"Okay, that's done." Matte turned to Damiano. "Toni, now do I pick up some sushi take out?"

"How about pasta? Sushi's cold; I want something warm, Pierre. On St-Laurent, you choose. You're out more than I am."

Matte complied, and Damiano went to freshen up with a little help as soon as they reached the restaurant. She took deep breaths and held them. "There's nothing wrong with me. Nothing." When she saw that Matte was sitting at a table, she joined him. "It's better we eat here." She went first for the bread. Matte didn't miss the ploy, but he didn't make any accusations.

"Slow down, Toni. Why do you eat like someone who's starving?"

"Because I am." She kept twirling her fork and spoon and waited impatiently for Matte to finish. "What do I owe you?"

"It's on the house."

"I'll get the next one. I'll just brush my teeth and be out in a flash."

"Keep your promise. No liquor in small bottles."

"I remember."

Connor Tibbett was already outside the Crémazie Division, waiting for Matte. The murder room was out, some detectives were still at work in the squad room, and Damiano's glass cage offered no privacy, so he chose the boardroom on the first floor and alerted Damiano. Tibbett sat on one side of the rectangular table and they on the other.

"At the time, Connor, you and your sister still lived at home?"

"Emma and I paid for our education, and my parents let us stay at home to help us out. But, on the night my parents died, I was the only one still at home because Emma was already married with kids."

"But you were both out that night, right?"

"Exam month. Emma was going to spend the night in Kirkland with her friend studying for her technician's exam, until I called her. I was at McGill cramming, but I suffer from migraines and got home earlier than I had planned."

"Was the front door unlocked?"

"Yes, and that was unusual. I had my keys out."

"Did you see your parents immediately?"

"No, I headed upstairs. I sensed that there was something off because my mother would have called me with, 'You're back.' Something like that. I came back down the stairs. I saw my father's leg first. I walked into the living room, and I couldn't comprehend what I was seeing. I froze before running over to them. I found no pulse, but they both seemed warm. Their clothes were soaked in blood. I wanted to call an ambulance right away, but I never understood what trauma was until I couln't move. All I could think of was that I had to breathe. When I finally called 9-1-1, I didn't recognize my high-pitched stuttering voice. Then I called Emma. She alerted her sitter and asked her to stay with the children until she was home. Emma's study friend drove her to my parents' place. When she arrived, we just held onto one another until the street filled with an ambulance, a fire truck and multiple police cars. Emma was allowed to go home to her children."

"What did you think occurred that night?" Damiano asked.

"A murder."

"Did it occur to you that it could have been a murder/suicide?"

"No, why would my father kill my mother? No."

"Were they happy together?"

"Who thinks about that? They were just my parents."

"Did they argue?"

"Yeah, I mean yes, but who doesn't argue with partners?"

"Did you think of looking for a weapon? Consider your answer carefully."

Connor looked away briefly, but they both caught the pause, which was an indication of a lie.

"No. Why would a killer leave his weapon behind? At least, I didn't see it and I didn't look. I kept my eyes on my parents."

"Was the coffee table overturned?"

"No."

"You see Connor, what concerns us is that there is no evidence of a struggle, no defense wounds, nothing awry or stolen. The only carpet prints were your parents and Emma's and yours. We also wonder if a killer shot your father, wouldn't your mother have tried to run away? Or vice versa."

"What if she was traumatized like me when I found them and just froze."

Matte jumped in. "You were frightened. Your mother or your father was facing death. Traumatized or not, she would have attempted to flee. Do you see the difference?"

"A female friend was attacked in a laundry room by a man. He was about to punch her in the face when someone walked in and he ran. She said she froze, didn't feel she was there, it was like a dream. Couldn't my mother have frozen too?"

"We're cops, Mr. Tibbett. When someone is murdered, we ask who benefits?"

"The killer who's gotten away with murder, that's who."

"What about you and your sister who inherited over a million dollars. The insurance policies wouldn't have paid out if the incident was a murder/suicide."

"Are you accusing me or Emma of killing our parents?" Tibbett got up from the table, kicking his chair, knocking it over, and headed for the door.

"Sit down Mr. Tibbett! For the moment, we think you might have taken the weapon. Then again, you and your sister could also be suspects."

"Damn you both."

Damiano concluded the interview. "We've finished for now, but we are only just beginning. We will learn what kind of relationship you had with each parent, and they with you."

Connor's eyes became slits, his lips thinned.

Damiano slid in another direction. "Did you want to be certain you'd receive the insurance money? It would have been so easy to get rid of the weapon. Or, maybe you didn't want it known that your father had shot your mother. When we have what we need, Mr. Tibbett, we will contact you."

"I thought you were here to help my sister and me to clear my father's name of the doubt that has plagued us for ten years. Instead, you're out to collar us. Isn't that the word you cops use?"

"Before you slam the door, was your father a gun owner?" Matte asked.

"He had two weapons. That doesn't mean anything. He hadn't hunted in years. Both guns were locked away in the basement."

"Could you identify them?"

"No. That's one of the reasons we… never mind." Connor slammed the door, the sound echoing down the hall.

CHAPTER EIGHT

As soon as Connor was safely inside his Mustang, he called his sister. "What's that commotion?"

"Nice hello, Connor. That's teenagers. There should be a special kind of hell reserved for them. You can't reason with them, they know everything, but when something goes wrong, it turns out to be my fault. I haven't time to talk, I'm refereeing. It's crazy because the house is big enough for all of us, but my big baby boys are always under foot."

The home on Broadview in Pointe Claire, a few doors down from the newly named Saint Thomas High School, was a sizeable old white brick and wood frame house that had four bedrooms and a finished basement. On the double lot, common in the area, her son Michael built and cared for a putting green in the spacious backyard. There was no reason for the continuous racket. But at least, Emma knew they were safe. When she'd driven over the traffic bumps in front of the school, she thought, "They didn't help the young student who tried to stop a fight and lost his life." At least, for the time being, her boys were secure.

"Emma!"

"I'm listening."

"This is serious, Sis. You have to make time."

"What's happened?" She asked in a high-pitch tremble.

"The police are reopening Mom and Dad's case. I just left the Major Crimes Division, and we seem to be their principal target."

"I have enough problems. I don't need this. Why can't they just leave us alone?"

"That noise is gawd-awful. Lock yourself in the bathroom or something."

"You think I'll be safe there?"

"You'll gain a few minutes, at least. Have you ever told anyone anything about Mom and Dad? Not even your friend Gina? I mean anything to anyone?"

"I have never said a word about Mom's so-called obsessions, but the kids sensed there was something off between me and Mom. Mom's need dominate led to a bad scene. The event or rumor, whatever it was, occurred twenty years ago though. I never knew the details or the truth. It's long forgotten. Rumors are lies with bits of truth. Leave it alone. Mom's long dead and her past with her."

"We have to get our stories straight. Don't mention that at all. Hope they don't go back that far. It's good some of those people are dead, we moved on. Dad never mentioned anything. We grew up, and the scars and rumors faded if they were ever true."

"Was there something else with Mom again?"

"I have no clue, Emma. My relationship with Dad is my problem. Don't go adding anything if they ask you."

"I'll just say there were ups and downs."

"You think they'll go for that?"

"Well, they won't believe I know nothing. I grew up with you."

"No specifics, then, Emma. I should never have called you the night they died. The police will check the phone logs and the time. Simple facts are not precise. It's been over ten years. We got off easy in the first two investigations. They all… all the detectives, believe I disposed of the weapon, and it was a murder/suicide."

"Connor, they have no proof. Even these new detectives won't be able to find proof. We stick to our stories. Good, the battle in the house has stopped. Let me open the door. Teenagers are sneaky, they might be huddled outside this door, listening." Emma opened the door very slowly and then whipped it open. "We're safe."

"Why do you think Dad had such antipathy for me?"

"Do you really want answers, Connor? First, and most important, I think Dad was very jealous of you."

"Why, for God's sake?"

"You're beautiful. I'm a Tibbett. You're some prince."

"That's bull."

"But true. He hated your freedom. No children, and no responsibilities."

"Was he that unhappy with his own life?"

"Who knows? I think he might have been disappointed that you were gay."

"I didn't choose any of it. Who would? Still hard, even today. The night they died I had this awful desire to let them rot. I could have left the house and done nothing."

"That's a horrid thing to say and what if someone had seen you at the house?"

"I stayed, Emma, and I did call 9-1-1. I have to trust you with something else."

"You know you can."

"Dad was still alive. He was wheezing for less than a minute. Then he stopped. Everything was quiet. I just stood there as though I were watching strangers, until I snapped out of the shock and called for help."

"I never knew you hated Mom and Dad."

"I didn't hate them – I felt nothing for them. I was eight when I knew I was different, and they sensed it too. I got birthday gifts I didn't want, and a few years later Dad made jokes aimed at me when we watched TV. A bike was the one gift I needed to get away as often as I could."

"I never knew about any of this."

"You were older and unaware. Anyway, it's all behind me now."

"I worry about the gun. The insurance money is long spent," Emma said. "I'd lose the house if I were forced to return it."

"They didn't find it for ten years. What chance do they have now? It's probably buried somewhere. Point is, it's long gone."

"Do you know where it is?"

"I was guessing. Of course, I don't know."

CHAPTER NINE

AFTER CONNOR TIBBETT left, Damiano and Matte began to plot the case on the cork boards. At the top of the first board they pinned photos of the victims and their children. Below, they placed the autopsy reports and brief notes of the trajectory of the bullet to Stu Tibbett's head. The forensic conclusion was that the trajectory was a match for a self-inflicted wound, or an assailant who had previously worked out and perfected the angle for this suicide shot. This position required practice, repeated practice to properly inflict such a wound. The forensic expert also felt the killer might have positioned his hand correctly by pretending it was a warning bluff. "If you do what I ask, no one will get hurt. We all walk away." The victim was frightened, hoped for the best and did not struggle. If indeed it was a double murder, it was callous and precise.

Beneath, they put up photo of the locus, photos from all angles and the entire room. The scene had an eerie simplicity, two victims, no fuss, no carnage.

The Barretts were placed on the second cork board of possible suspects and photos of acquaintances who were previously questioned, neighbors, colleagues. Damiano and Matte didn't pin any notes, but their addresses and cell numbers, until they questioned these people themselves.

"Let's call it a night. You have to go home sometime, Toni."

"I've changed my mind. I need some Ativan. Would you give me a few? The minute I stop working, my nerves twist and pull."

"You don't have to go through this with just me. Jeff loves you."

"And can suffocate me at the same time. This is my life – I want to make the choices, even if I'm wrong. I can't listen to his litany of other cases: their diets, sleep routines, breathing exercises and medical reports. I just don't have the energy for Jeff's love. This is something I have to face on my own. I don't have lung cancer until the PET scan. Look, I'm already having trouble breathing."

"Alright Toni, I carry one with me, but I won't give you more than one a day. And no alcohol with it."

"Thanks. Pierre. You carry one with you?"

"One never knows."

"True."

Damiano carefully hid the Ativan in a Kleenex. She white-knuckled the steering wheel on the drive home. Wine was the answer. A glass of wine with one tablet wouldn't be a problem. Matte was too cautious. The house was quiet. Luke was probably studying, and she found Jeff engrossed in another biography. She couldn't make out the subject.

"I know I'm late, but it's a brutal, complex case."

Jeff rose to greet Damiano. "I'm just glad you're home. Can I make you something?"

"I'd die for a large glass of wine and a grilled cheese the way you make it."

"Coming up. Take my chair because I've warmed it up for you. I'll pour the wine."

While Jeff was busy, she took out the tissue and retrieved the tiny pill.

"Here we go, my sweet."

"I'm thirsty and I'm starving. Muchas gracias. I'm just beat."

As soon as Jeff was out of the room, Damiano placed the pill on her tongue and took a heavy swig of wine, and then another.

"I saw that."

Damiano jumped, almost spilling the wine. "You've taken up lurking, Luke. It was an aspirin for a headache."

"I didn't mean to scare you. I came down for food."

"Don't spy!"

"Sorry, alright?"

"How was your exam yesterday?"

"Difficult but doable. The profs have taken to asking questions on material they've never taught."

"Bummer."

"Aptly put. Now, I need to eat. Goodnight."

"Good luck tomorrow."

"Thanks, but I don't need it."

"Lucky you."

Damiano finished her wine and waited for whatever drowsiness would embrace her. She knew she couldn't consume the grilled cheese or she'd feel nothing. The sandwich would dilute the effect of the pill. Toni had to stall before eating it, let the Ativan do its thing. When Jeff appeared at the door with the sandwich, she had to find a way to stall. "Thanks for this. How was your day?"

Jeff stood holding the grilled cheese, pleased with Toni's interest. "Crazy busy. With the pandemic slowdown, every mother wants her child checked, needlessly most of them. Add anxiety, bedlam which children easily cause 24/7 and boredom, and you have twitchy, anger-prone mothers. It seems everyone is angry." Jeff reached over and poured more wine. "Last glass. The sandwich is getting cold."

Damiano could feel her anxiety fading. Heavy and sleepy, she rose and said, "I'll bring it up with me. I am beat. Love you and thanks."

"No kiss?"

"My kingdom for a bed. We never stopped all day. I'll be with it tomorrow, promise." She didn't bother to brush her teeth. Sleep slowly erased the thought of cancer.

At six-fifteen, the first sensation that Damiano felt was being pinioned. On the verge of striking out, she realized it was Jeff's arm around her waist. Gently, she lifted his arm and rolled free.

"I'm awake," he mumbled. "You were lost to the world, too much wine."

"I was bushed." She almost stepped on the dried grilled cheese and realized she hadn't taken a bite. She pushed it under the bed and she'd attend to it later.

Jeff sat up. "You still look tired. Are you okay?"

"I had one of my signature dreams where I'm lost and I spend the dream trying to find a way out."

"Are you stressed about something?"

"I'm just a tortured soul. These dreams tire me out because they color my day and linger." She couldn't believe she was hung over from one Ativan. Well, two large glasses of wine didn't help.

"I'll whip you up scrambled eggs, toast and coffee while you shower."

"I don't deserve you."

"Sometimes true. I have to rush, busy day too."

CHAPTER TEN

DAMIANO ARRIVED AT WORK early, but Matte was already adding maps to the cork board and scanning the information. "Did you have a good night's sleep?"

"Cancer never entered my thoughts or dreams."

"Good to hear."

"As I drove, I began to have second thoughts about us even considering Barrett as a potential suspect. I admit I didn't study both cases as assiduously as you."

"I've given both of them a good deal of thought. On the surface, they make good money and don't need to ruin their lives again. What does Brian Barrett gain by murdering the couple? He said his wife was still on shaky ground. My mother knew a large family whose son was killed in a DUI. Although they still had seven children and weren't alone, the wife never recovered and died five years later of a broken heart. Doctors are finally legitimizing broken hearts. Mothers don't recover from the loss of a child. Think what it must be like to feel responsible for your toddler's death. I would guess she's still in therapy.

"Now to the money. The Tibbetts literally stole $150,000 from her when she was crushed with grief, and they boasted about the sale. Boasted! That money would have almost doubled in 2012. It could have been used to help pay for the dental clinic and its equipment. Instead, his parents gave a little help, but he was working long hours to earn a salary. It takes about five years to pay off the overhead. His wife lost their child and their money. Forgiving oneself is almost impossible. Barrett had a wife, and they had a second child, Piper, that he himself almost lost, so he couldn't blame her. He knew he'd lose everything if he did. There was the anger and the misery of losing his only son that he could never fully shift the liability to his wife. He turned all his anger and vengeance on the Tibbetts. He's a smart man who felt he could avenge his family and evade the law. Actually, maybe he has."

"It's all about money then?" Toni said.

"Money and loss. We'll have a better sense of the Barretts when we interview both of them and then a clearer view of what we are dealing with."

"Ten years to harbor enough anger to murder?" Toni questioned.

"Anger and hatred can fester for years. It can also become distorted."

"I get the point. Even so," Toni pointed out, "that's a delicate situation, and we're banking on supposition. We should dig into the Tibbetts first. We have a list of friends and possible enemies. Good grist for us. We need to find out who they were. Their children were of no help. Both previous investigations have ruled out gambling debts, a rap sheet and fraud. We begin with Stu Tibbett. What was his motive? What drove him to murder his wife and take his own life? Every family has secrets they'd protect from fear of exposure. We have to discover what they were in this family."

"There was actually more information on her. She was a snoop, craved attention, betrayed friends' trust and was ambitious. Those comments came from her colleagues. Toni, we should go at her together. I've discovered people you'd never suspect of infidelity are the worst offenders. She also applied for the special needs principal job and failed. The woman must have her good points, but she definitely possessed another side as do I," Matte added.

"Let's see what the daughter can tell us. From there we go to friends and enemies."

CHAPTER ELEVEN

It was rare that Emma Tibbett received calls at work because, except for emergencies, it was against company policy. That it was her ex, caught her off guard and she picked up.

"Look Emma, I know you're working, but I'm flush and I thought you might like to get the child allowance early."

"The casino?"

"Yep. Three thousand four hundred! Can I drop off the money or maybe even have a bite together tonight?"

Emma didn't want to eat with him ever again, but the cash support usually late was always needed. "Sure. In Pointe Claire Village?"

"Le Gourmand around six."

"See you then." The second call followed on the heels of the first. A shiver rolled across her shoulders when she saw that the number was unlisted. "Emma Tibbett."

"Lieutenant Detective Damiano."

"My brother informed me you are reopening my parents' case."

"We are. In point of fact, it was never closed."

"I see."

"We'd like you to come to the division and go over the information you have already given, and possibly, something you might have unwittingly forgotten."

"When?"

"Two o'clock today. Do you need the address?"

"No, I've been there three times. Detective, this is really not convenient. I have to inform my colleagues and miss my patient for his MRI unless another specialized tech is available."

"You are a specialized technician then?"

"A busy one."

"Your colleagues will understand this is a police matter."

"I can't think of anything I might add to the case."

"You'd be surprised what people remember, given time." Damiano sat with notes from the first investigation. She set the time for the appointment with Emma Tibbett.

Damiano looked over at Matte and continued. "I want the names of colleagues who knew Carol Tibbett at the time of the sale for any additional information they might have shared. Sometimes we share more with people we work with every day than with friends under the assumption it's safer. I also want names of people around the time of her death. Something might have happened, a row, a discovery, something."

"I have made mine," Matte said as soon as his calls were completed.

"Of course. Why would I be surprised?"

"I may surprise you yet. I'm taking you to my favorite curry resto on St-Laurent Street. You're stressed and you need a break from our routine."

"Do you think I have cancer, Pierre?"

"I've read up on the early symptoms: persistent cough, shortness of breath, hoarseness, chest pain and blood from dry coughing. You have none of those."

"Yes, but if the oncologist caught it early, I wouldn't yet, would I. Did you remember the Ativan?"

"One way or the other, I'm stuck with you, and I have the Ativan."

"Thanks, Pierre."

"You'd do the same for me."

"I would. Let's do an early lunch."

"If Tibbett shot his wife and himself, he had a reason. That's what we have to find," Matte said. "The daughter might not be able to help, but we'll give it a try."

When they were back at the division, Damiano was still twitchy. "Let's take the stairs."

"It's six floors."

Matte sent an officer down to meet Tibbett and escort her to the boardroom which offered privacy. Tibbett was older than the photo and taller than expected. The woman was not attractive, but she knew how to make the best use of makeup and simplicity. Her dress was beige, and she wore a short blue stylish sweater. She had a tight smile during the introductions, but that was to be expected under the circumstances. Her rimless glasses made her small eyes appear larger.

Damiano began. "Detective Matte and I are endeavoring to discover the reason two people were summarily shot and killed. Our investigation of your father revealed nothing remarkable: no gambling, no debts, no serious infractions, or enemies we could locate. This is a difficult question, but I must ask it. Did your father ever sexually interfere with you?"

Blood rushed to Tibbett's cheeks. "How dare you? No! Never!" She started to rise and thought better of it. "My father is the victim."

Matte took over to settle the charged atmosphere, and inadvertently added to it. "Your brother told us of his animosity to both parents, especially your father."

"I'm not a homophobe, but I understand my father's disappointment, knowing his name would not carry on, and that..."

"His son was gay," Matte added.

"Yes. My father was often unkind, and my brother purposely flaunted his sexuality. The dual hostility never rose to the level of murder. Connor made sure he was rarely home."

Damiano went back to hard points. "The words used to describe your mother are harsh: ruthless and disloyal. Her ambition often led to failures. I won't list them. We sense your mother was a very angry woman."

"She was a good mother and unfortunately very insecure. She told me once there was so much pressure to marry young and do the right thing when she was young that she settled. That in itself is not unusual, even today. She merited more. And she went after it, and failed. I know about the Manresa Court home. And I am ashamed. My mother was better than such an opportunist. We all reach a point in our lives where we have to admit we thought we'd be more successful or more mature... I didn't want to settle, so I married a 'bad boy'. Too soon, I had two children and another on the way. Pretty boy left, and I spend part of each month fighting for child support. That's life as they say."

"Did you know that the penalty for obstruction of justice is two years of incarceration and a five thousand dollar fine?" Damiano spoke very slowly.

Emma was flustered and did not mean to blurt out, "I didn't touch the gun."

Damiano smiled briefly, but followed the lead gifted to her. "If your brother..."

"He didn't. I know nothing about the gun." Emma knew she had caught herself in the mess. "All the other detectives drilled us, it seemed forever, about the gun. They confiscated my father's two old rifles that were locked in the basement of the house."

"Can you think of anything your mother might have done to get herself killed?"

"No. I can't. I have to go."

"Before you do, I want you to give some deep thought about your situation. Matte and I can't find the people responsible for the deaths of children in the residential schools across Quebec and the rest of the country, or the mass shootings in the States, or the atrocities occurring in Ukraine, but we intend to discover how a modest suburban couple met their death. We owe justice to the victims, and if that means we come down hard on you and your brother, we will, I promise you. Neither one of you has been completely honest. Rethink your answers. They were your parents for God's sake. Here's my private cell number." Damiano handed over her card.

CHAPTER TWELVE

Emma Tibbett hurried from the division feeling frantic. The other detectives had shown perhaps a pseudo kindness, but Damiano and Matte's directness rattled her very being. She called Connor, hoping this was a day he worked from home.

"Donegani and Tibbett."

"It's me. I have to see you. I've just been questioned by those two detectives."

Connor's nerves tightened behind his shoulder blades. "You didn't tell them anything?"

"No, but they seem to already know something. They suspect us. They know we haven't told them everything we know. They swore they'd come down hard."

"Alright, calm down. I'm home working. I have to tell you that Timothy and I split."

"Really? You were close friends since McGill. You spent what, eleven years together? That's almost a lifetime."

"The last seven we were roommates. He packed his things, and drove back to his condo in Delray, Florida, in his Mini Cooper. We spent some of the winter there. I was done, but he wanted to hang on."

"Did you part on good terms?"

"Whoever does? No matter how you view it, parting is a failure."

"I'm sorry."

"Don't be. I'm not. You know how to get here, right?"

"Grand Boulevard?"

"The same. Number four. Take Sherbrooke Street."

Emma was still jittery. The stress settled in her back. Clicking on her Bluetooth, Emma gave the verbal command: "Call Devon." He picked up quickly. "Can we make that seven-thirty? I'm really caught up here."

"Of course. I'm at your disposal."

Despite the stress, Emma almost laughed at the old charm as she drove into Notre-Dame-de-Grace, one of the city's most popular multicultural neighborhoods, leafy and friendly in summer and fall. Yet, Emma felt a growing fear. She found Grand easily. It wasn't far from the Loyola University campus. Connor's condo building was a red brick, two-story building nicely recessed from the sidewalk with freshly budding trees that softened the noise from Sherbrooke Street, the busy main thoroughfare. Parking anywhere in the city wasn't easy, the reason more and more city residents didn't drive. She hesitated before she buzzed. The door unlocked immediately, and Connor was standing by his open door, waiting for her.

Emma envied the quiet of his place and the neatness. Connor himself smelled as fresh as his morning shower. As a senior financial advisor, he'd done very well during the pandemic, and Connor didn't deprive himself. His one steady asset was his condo. He'd bought his art in Old Montreal. His colors were gray and pale yellow, and his furniture, uncomfortable but stylish. "Begin at the beginning, but first tell me you divulged nothing."

"Nothing, I promise. I can't stay too long because I'm having dinner with Devon. He finally has the back child support to give me. I'm meeting him seven-thirty."

"What a loser!"

"At least Devon's paying up. I made the blunder of thinking marriage would change him. Connor, the whole time I was with the police I was thinking of what you'd told me. Why didn't you help Dad?"

"My answer for you is simply, I didn't want to. I was in shock. I also thought he would die any second. He was bleeding from his nose and mouth."

"Why didn't you attempt CPR, you were a licensed lifeguard?"

"I wanted him to die. Would you willingly care for him? He'd have permanent brain damage. Would you be up for that?" There was a sudden chill in the room. "Would you? I know I wasn't."

"It's so cold-blooded."

"I wasn't thinking clearly that night. I was in shock."

"Connor, I know you took the gun. The cops do too."

"They'd have arrested me by now if they did, if they had any proof. Your nerves are getting the better of you, Emma."

"The police told me the penalty for obstruction of justice is prison time – two years, and a five thousand dollar fine. We'd both lose our livelihoods. Then, try to find another job after prison. They vowed to go after us mercilessly."

"You're hysterical!"

"No, I'm not. You took that gun, didn't you?"

"You don't need to know." Connor was shouting now.

"I do. You let Dad die without even the weakest attempt to help him. You took that gun, not to protect their reputation, but for the money."

"How dare you? You think I never noticed you had a strange relationship with Dad?"

"You're just jealous that he was more attentive to me. I admit he was probably disappointed with you, and I received a double scoop of affection."

Connor sneered. "Was it more than that?"

"Are you trying to create a motive for me to deflect one from yourself?"

"You're nuts! Keep your secrets. I'm not a snitch. Em, I don't even know what I did that night. I was in shock. I couldn't move even if I'd wanted to. I don't think I was as bad as I'm telling you – fuck! I was in shock."

"I have one more question." Emma was edging toward the door. "Did you murder Mom and Dad, Connor? Did you hate them that much?" When Emma reached the door, she ran down the hall.

Connor began to run after her, and stopped. The vein at his temple bulged and throbbed "She's not that stupid."

It was only when she was hunched over, trying to breathe, that Emma remembered her date for the child support. She fumbled in her purse till she located the number and called. "Devon, I am so sorry. I was with the police and that's why you've had to wait."

"You sound awful. I've walked around the village, checked out the yacht club, sat by the water with my thoughts and now I'm on my second glass of wine. I'm enjoying people watching. Do you still need a sympathetic ear?"

"Have you developed one?"

"I'll work on it till you arrive."

When Emma saw herself in the car mirror, she could see the stress in her eyes and mouth. "What a mess!"

Luckily, she found parking in the lot across from Le Gourmand on St-Anne Street in Pointe Claire Village. The old stone home with the brown shutters always looked to her as if with each year it sank a little more into the ground. When she walked inside, its white linen table cloths, red leather chairs and stone walls created an atmosphere of old Quebec. The kitchen aromas swept one into a simpler past.

Devon rose to greet her and her heart did a small leap. *Why do men look even better with age?* He hugged her long and hard. "First things first, let me give you the money and a little extra for Michael's graduation before I lose it. I'll order my shrimp with Cajun sauce. What will you have?"

"I'll have the potage du jour, their pea soup, comforting and warm."

"Now, what's going on?" His dark hair was graying at the temples giving him validity he didn't have, while his deep dimples were still boyish. "Police?"

"A new team has reopened Mom and Dad's case. The two detectives are strongly suggesting that we took the gun and disposed of it for the money."

"Can't you see through that, Emma?"

"What do you mean? They're threatening us with obstruction and prison time."

"It's a bluff. Cops threaten, cajole, befriend and lie to apprehend their targets. If Connor admits he took the gun, bingo bango, case solved with little effort. Murder/suicide. Gold stars. Connor pleads shock, he does community service. I work security now, so I know a few things."

"They have unnerved us both to a point where Connor and I are accusing one another."

"Stick to your stories. Offer up nothing. They can't prove anything. The first two investigations couldn't, they won't either."

"You make it all so simple."

"I'm looking at it from the outside."

You're not implicated.

"You're a good woman, Emma. Tell me again why you left me?"

The initial battles of Devon's gambling, debts and the occasional beat-downs from his debtors had all been lost. His charm and good nature belied his failures. How Devon could work in a good job at the

Montreal Casino and then travel across the border to the Mohawk Casino and gamble that salary at a Native casino had worn her down. Emma was too preoccupied with her present worries and chose to keep her answer simple. "Money and trouble with zippers."

CHAPTER THIRTEEN

ONCE EMMA TIBBETT left the station, Matte noticed that Damiano was deep in thought, so he interrupted, guessing what it was. "A harried suspect serves us well. The brother and sister will argue, and something will fall out."

Damiano's phone buzzed and she delayed before picking up. "Lieutenant Detective Damiano." Matte could see her whole body tense. "I'd rather wait."

"Detective, we are in the middle of a pandemic. We'd like you to come in for your PET scan. You're one of the lucky ones. Many sick, worried patients can't even get an appointment. We take good care of our patients. No fasting is required. You'll need a hospital card. See you at eight-fifteen tomorrow." The receptionist had hung up before Damiano had a chance to postpone the appointment.

"Who does that woman think she is? I should call and cancel the whole thing."

"But you won't because you're scared but intelligent."

"Why did this have to happen?"

"Let's not start that. What time do they want you there?"

"I need to get a hospital card before eight-fifteen."

"Do you want me to pick you up at home?"

"Are you nuts? Jeff will smell something. I've told you I don't want Jeff knowing anything until it's over. I'll be at the office at six-thirty, so we can have an early start. Pierre, I won't forget this."

"I know. Do you need the rest of the day off?"

"NO! I don't want any time to think."

"Let me take your mind off this, Toni. I have the name of a guy who taught with Tibbett for years. I'll call him. The back story on Tibbett will begin with him. You should look for the woman who taught with Carol Tibbett for the same reason for her."

"Why don't we work together on this, Pierre. I don't want to work alone."

"I just thought a man would more easily open up to another man."

"Leave your phone open; I'll listen in the car. It's another favor."

"I'm okay with that."

"I know I'll be less productive, but I might just pick up on something you miss."

Matte made the call and luckily found the friend at home in Pierrefonds. "Phil Clendening is retired with 'lots of time on my hands." They were both quiet on the drive to the West Island. Matte knew Damiano needed time to herself. Everything had occurred so quickly. Matte felt that was good, less time to brood.

Once they found the house, they sat in the living room with coffee. "How does one sum up a guy you worked with but never really knew. I was thinking how odd that was waiting for you. There are hierarchies in every school. There are the select few reputed to be the best teachers, the herd of journeymen and the slouches and plotters who spend a lot of time cozying up to the admin. Stu was a journeyman, a solo, a man who was present in groups, but never center. I think he said what he thought people wanted to hear. Privately pompous I felt."

"I gather you never knew if he engaged in extracurricular activities?"

"No, I never was that intimate with him. I just remembered, it's odd, but he liked gossip. Perhaps that's not odd, men gossip as much as women."

"Did he ever mention his wife?"

"He must have, but nothing sticks."

"Did he have a temper?"

"He sulked. My wife used to say she was glad I was loud; it was the quiet men she couldn't trust. Anyway, whatever Stu was, he didn't deserve to die."

"So, you can't imagine him murdering his wife, then shooting himself."

"I can't be forthcoming about such a tragedy – they're both long dead. I leave them in peace. My wife died four years ago. I wish she were still around even it was just to nag me. Freedom is not what we think it'll be. That's it for me. I try not to think of sadness."

In the car on the way to the division, Matte asked, "Well Toni, what do you think?"

"An everyman, a loner, a quiet sulker and a gossip can explode given the right reason."

"That's what we have to find, a reason."

CHAPTER FOURTEEN

ON HER WAY HOME THAT afternoon, Damiano had missed a message from Jeff. He had an unscheduled meeting and he expected to be home a little after nine. "What luck! I won't have to hide my feelings and I'll be in bed early, courtesy of the Ativan and wine." She went to the kitchen and poured herself a healthy glass of wine.

"What's up with you, Mom? You've hardly talked to Dad or me all week."

Damiano was as angry as she was scared. "I'm just out of sorts, Luke."

"If I pulled that bull on you, I'd never get away with it. Something's up."

"I'm on an ugly case, and Matte and I are the third team to work it. So far, we have nothing, and the people involved are blocking our efforts."

"That's not it."

When had Luke gone from being a teenager to a perceptive young man? "Just let it go for a couple of days, Luke? I have to figure this out on my own."

"Have you considered I might be able to help?"

"Luke, you can help by not sharing your doubts with your father and giving me some space. It seems to me you've asked me for space a few times. I need to be alone."

He left the kitchen in a hurry. That was the boy she recognized. She ran to the foot of the stairs and called up. "Luke, you can really help me by making me two sandwiches and taking them to the bedroom. I'll shower and make it an early night."

"What kind?" he shouted through the door.

"Surprise me."

The wine bottle went up to the bedroom as well. Damiano stripped and left her clothes in a pile on the chair. She stood in the shower blasting the hot spray to loosen her back muscles. She stood naked while she dried her thick hair which was always a proud chore, except that night. She quickly donned her terrycloth robe and dug into her purse for the Kleenex and its booty which she hid under her pillow. She hid the bottle of wine too. Luke was a snoop like her.

"Is it safe to enter?" Luke asked.

"Of course. Two egg salad on whole wheat. Perfect!" she said.

"Do what you have to do, but I'm just a shout away."

Before he could move, Damiano deposited a big sloppy kiss on Luke's cheek.

"I'm outta here."

With help, she was asleep before Jeff got home and gone before he was up. Her note read: "Love you much. See you tonight."

Matte was waiting for her. "You okay?"

"Next question."

"We'll go in from Pine Avenue. I'll park while you get the hospital card. Turn right at the first corridor. The office is at the end on your right. I'll wait for you at the snack bar you'll see to the left of the entrance."

"How do you know all this?"

"My mother's stroke."

"Right."

When Damiano passed the hospital chapel, she recalled praying for her friend there, in the back pew. She immediately recalled the six flights of stairs she ran up every day to sit quietly beside Leslie in her room. Tears fell before she knew she was crying. *I do not have cancer! So, dry up.* The hospital was like Grand Central Station and the staff were no amateurs. It was all business. Even the patients walking the hall pushing their saline bags had a definite beat. A warm comfort spread over her when she saw Matte and she threw her arms around him.

"Pretty lady, you're not my type."

"Oh you! I have to find the room number." She reached in the pocket of her camel jacket. "Damn! I forgot it."

"We can ask the first nurse or orderly we see." They were led to a smaller room than Damiano recalled.

A nurse handed her a blue hospital gown. "Keep your bra and pants and put your clothes in this plastic bag and carry it with you. Follow me when you're done." She turned to Matte. "Sir, I'll direct you to the waiting room." Damiano surrendered control, since there was no other choice. The room was claustrophobic, but she spotted Saku Koivu's name on the wall, the Montreal Canadiens' hockey captain who had donated the PET scan during his battle with cancer. When she was finally ushered into the immediate waiting room, the nurse's table was less than three feet from the curtained bed and chair that corralled her. She couldn't see the scan because of the curtain. One hour past her appointed time, the nurse called over. "Sorry for the delay, we have an emergency." Two hours later still no one had appeared. In the third hour, four nurses very slowly pushed a gurney that grazed her chair with a poor man, semi-conscious and skeletal, into the scan room.

That's dying. Damiano didn't move a muscle when they wheeled him out. The nurse finally came to her with a sizeable glass of white liquid. "Drink it all. You're up in thirty minutes. Someone has spoken to your husband, he's very worried."

Damiano made no comment and, thirty-five minutes later, walked into the room and positioned herself on the clean towels put down on the scanner bed for her. She closed her eyes. The scan was over in a few minutes. She dressed behind the curtain, pulling her clothes from the bag, and asked the nurse. "Will I be called with the results?"

"God, no. Too busy for that. Your doctor will have them in about ten days to two weeks."

Matte rose to greet her.

"The scan is nothing. The results are everything. Okay, husband, we can drive back to the office."

"Ha, ha. I didn't correct them either."

"I'll never be able to thank you enough."

"That's the best part!"

Damiano elbowed Matte in the ribs.

"Food?"

"I never ate the sandwiches Luke made for me last night. Should we go to the Orange Julep? I love our fabled Montreal restaurant built and painted like an orange."

"Junk food now?"

"Toasted dogs, fries and a Julep. You have to let yourself go, Pierre. I have a real story to tell you. Make sure you drive up the service road to the Julep because it's impossible to make a right or left turn into the Julep. You end up driving in circles. Well, here goes. An old Jewish woman had her assisted death papers signed and her date chosen. Her neighbor, my cousin, went to say her good-byes. Maureen gets a call the next day from Sarah. She figures it's her son to tell her everything went well. When Maureen hears Sarah's voice, she jumps."

"'I delayed my death for a week. I need a favor from you. Would you buy and cook me a half pound of bacon? When you're done, ask for me, don't let the nurses see or smell what you have, or they will confiscate it.'

"Trying not to snort, Maureen agrees and follows through. Sarah calls a few hours later. 'Thank you, Maureen. One of my biggest regrets is that I didn't eat bacon all my life. In the end, which is where I'm at, rules are bullshit!'"

"Julep, it is. I agree."

"Makes you think."

"It does."

CHAPTER FIFTEEN

ONCE THEY WERE SUGARED up and in the murder room, Damiano found the list she wanted and announced to Matte that an Elizabeth Healy who taught with Carol Tibbett in 1998 and onwards lived in Dorval on Dawson Avenue. They called Healy first, and her husband answered. "Don't tell me Beth has gotten herself into some trouble. It's too late in the game for such things. She's at Costco and she should be home any minute. She's been there for more than an hour already. Here's her cell number."

"What is this about, Detective? I'm on my way home."

"Carol Tibbett."

"Still?"

"We need some answers."

"I'll be home shortly, but I don't know how I can help."

Damiano and Matte knew what they wanted to ask, and within the hour, they were parking in front of a home almost concealed by trees and a mass of pesky squirrels. Healy was a heavy woman with an easy smile. The detectives were glad to get to safety inside the cluttered house. "Those damn squirrels can fly at you, Pierre."

"Well, not now."

"Can I get you something?" It was asked with the hope that the answer was 'no'.

Damiano went for the main question. "Is there anything, Mrs. Healy, you didn't disclose to the first investigations that might help us understand why her husband would murder his wife?"

Healy dropped her head. "Yes, but I didn't want to sully Carol's reputation. She was already dead, so, in my books, I let her be."

"Well now we need to know."

"She wasn't the only teacher who frolicked with Ted Bouchard who taught gym. Please understand that I have no actual proof, just hearsay."

"Frolicked?"

"There was a ski trip for the children each winter. At night, Ted would disappear with one of the teachers and turn up all frisky in the morning with the pretence they skied all night and fell asleep on the hill. Ted never even bothered to change his story. There was no proof, but I was a math teacher, so I can add. Ted can't help you now, stomach cancer got him."

"Do you think her husband might have discovered their escapade?"

"No idea. I'm not certain she had one. You should talk to Eva Larson. Carol was loud and talkative. Eva taught beside her for many years. Eva moved to Le Cambridge retirement home. I have her number. She's a lovely woman and a golfer. I'll call her for you. It's her bridge day, so she ought to be there.

"Eva. You'll have company in an hour. Police. No, it's not for parking tickets."

"Good! Tell them to go to the main desk."

"Thanks. How do you live with the squirrels?"

"We have a peace bond."

"What a character!" Pierre said, as they drove along the Trans-Canada Highway to their exit at St. John's Boulevard. Eva was at the front counter. She was a tall, slender woman who'd let her hair go a silver white. Her movement, with a cane, was graceful. They followed her to her apartment.

"The halls are long and they seem to be getting longer. The Cambridge always reminds me of an assembly line. You saw the three, huge buildings. That said, my daughter found me an apartment, in the back, facing Seigniory Avenue. The lawns back here are lovely, and I made three friends. The coffee shop is my haven, two lattes and a heated carrot muffin with melting butter. I'm quite happy. I ignore the walkers, and wheelchairs."

Damiano smiled. She liked the woman. Mrs. Larson made tea without asking and set out a plate of delicious, tiny home-made muffins. Damiano wanted to stuff a couple in her pocket.

"My daughter made those."

Pierre began, "We know about the ski nights, the failures to secure posts Tibbett wanted. We need something new, and Mrs. Healy directed us to you."

"Darn her, she would. Well, our principals were a motley collection of males, some of the time not terribly intelligent, but they ruled back then. We hit one out of the park, let me see, that was 1998. I'm no good with dates, so you have to trust me. James Hughes was transferred to our school and stole every woman's heart. Hollywood handsome, a meticulous dresser, gentle and kind, not perfect, but good, *a bona homme*. It didn't take long for teachers to hang out in his office. Later they said he had favorites, he didn't seek them out, to me. I felt, it was the other way around. Women always found a reason to go to his office.

"Carol was smitten and got her nerve up to invite him to lunch. Carol liked to command. Perhaps, smitten isn't right. She might have wanted Hughes to do as she asked. She liked things her way. I heard her news because she told her best friend so loudly, I could hear every word. An hour later, her door slammed. They were both married, for heaven's sake. Carol, not to be deterred, tried again a week later – a door slammed louder. A few weeks later, I heard Carol say the damn card had cost her eleven twenty-nine and 'he just better'. I learned from Eva that James accepted, but invited two other teachers along.

"When I saw her that afternoon, she was so angry and hurt her eyes were slits. 'I'll show him!' When I went home, she was still in her classroom. I peeked in and she was busy with a letter. She confided to her friend she'd sent it to the new administrator, appointed from Montreal. She accused Hughes of carrying an open wine bottle to a party in the lunch room after school but while a student was still in school, or something close to that. We had an afternoon party for teachers, but what I heard made James sound incompetent. Such celebrations were common practices in other schools. Sending this letter to a new admin who didn't know James was intended to get back at him. I wasn't brave enough to contradict her and admit I was eavesdropping. To this day, I regret my cowardice, but Carol was blustery. She may never have sent the letter.

"Everybody knew James had cancer. He'd had two surgeries, but he never talked about them. He was determined to keep working. The story was that Carol may have written additional letters, but rumors were rampant. No one really knew the facts. You should talk to his widow who soon retired and took up art, water colors. She's had Montreal exhibitions. She'd remember the tragic events better than I. I have one of her art pieces, St-Joachim church. Its simplicity is striking. I don't have her number, but she has a website and is all over the net."

"Thanks, I'll put it on my phone," Damiano said.

"All manner of rumors spread devouring his career."

CHAPTER SIXTEEN

"Suburbia and teachers are not the dullards we thought!" Damiano almost laughed.

"Scratch any surface."

"Right you are. Sandra Hughes? Here she is in Pointe Claire. Living in Southwest One, and I have a number." Matte made the call, she answered on the fourth ring. "Detective Matte of Major Crimes."

"Is this some kind of joke?"

Matte explained.

"I'd rather not be involved, but I suppose I am by default."

Matte gave Hughes the directions and suggested eleven o'clock the next day.

"I have a CBC interview around eight. Can we make the appointment earlier?"

"How about ten?"

"I'll be there, reluctantly."

Damiano was too friendly with Jeff at dinner, and he was beginning to smell a rat, but she went on about suburbia and made certain she never gave him a chance to ask any questions. Then she was off with a good kiss on his mouth, and he made plans to get to the truth that night. He'd been taken, but not for long.

Matte and Damiano sat in the murder room, pinned a photo of Sandra Hughes to the wall and listened to Sonali Karnick of CBC radio Montreal interview Hughes. "They're both quick and funny like they know one another," Damiano said.

"They probably do," Matte added. "I'll meet her downstairs." He saw Hughes walking towards the door, and not for the first time he thought, *Women! You never know what to expect.* She didn't resemble his idea of an artist or a former teacher. With tight fitting navy Roots sports leg wear, a knitted blue Patagonia sweater jacket and Air27C Nike sport shoes, she looked like a high-powered coach. Her light brown curly hair appeared natural, and her green/blue eyes took one right on without a blink. For a woman in her sixties, she was as fit as an athlete. *Wait till Toni sees the shoes!*

"It was a good interview," Matte said, after he and Damiano had listened to it.

"Sonali makes it easy."

"We're on the sixth floor."

"Let's walk then."

Damiano was waiting at the elevator when she saw the door open, and she joined them and introduced herself. She asked Hughes if she was comfortable in the murder room.

"I'm fine. I'll sit with my back to the photos. This is the last place I wanted to be."

Damiano didn't miss the shoes, but decided to leave them until the end of the questioning. The details and the information thus far she shared with Hughes. "Do you recall what you were doing the night of the murder/suicide?"

"Ten years ago? I was home, probably on the phone. The crime took place on a week day, I think. I celebrate weekends. The police didn't identify the Tibbetts for a couple of days. You can check the phone logs."

"Did you keep your husband's case files?"

"For nine years, I did. I knew them by heart. They were painful reminders of James and what he went through, so I finally tore them up sheet by sheet and threw them out."

"The letters?"

"They were repetitive insinuations. James demanded that he be allowed to face the accuser because they never officially identified her, but he was never given the opportunity, never! He was forty-eight when his life met a fork in the road, and he was pulled down both lanes. Cancer and his livelihood. As an aside, two years after James died, I learned that that woman went after another colleague. The admin, I learned, returned to the post she'd held before the promotion. My principal had been very kind during James's illness and told me to bring me some of the letters the woman had sent. I had kept five of the seven. Well, the letter he showed me was a match for this new attack against an excellent teacher, so alike, all one had to do was change the name.

"They are identical in every point. Unfortunately, it's too late. Poor James. I was about to shred this letter, but here, you might need it someday," the principal said and handed the letter.

"On both fronts. That should have happened with all of these letters. Once any kind of indictment begins, one is caught in the gears. James was called in for his yearly evaluation. Principals prepared their own evaluations and they were signed by the head admin. There were three boxes: very satisfactory, satisfactory, and unsatisfactory. She checked the top box and signed. James was flummoxed and told a few friends. School gossip travels faster than prison news. The next afternoon a very formal letter was hand delivered, charging James with forgery. We had hired a lawyer by then, the wrong one. An educational lawyer knew the game. We had signed with a lawyer suggested to us who was not familiar with educational process. Lawyers have their games. 'We'll win hands down.' Later, 'we need more money. The file is more complicated than I thought.' A month later, an RCMP forensic specialist pronounced the signature authentic. We thought the case was over. Gears.

"They followed with the next charge. Allowing three teachers time off to make hospital visits or important appointments. The teachers would hire their own substitutes, certified teachers, and pay them and their absence would not be reported. To the board, the practice was wrong, but common in special circumstances. Cancer was involved in both of James's cases. The schoolboard knew about these breaches, but never took action. James was summoned and demoted.

"This time the admin, perhaps under pressure herself, was determined to prove her bones. She demanded that James produce receipts for every dollar spent with the year's budget. James said he had a drawer full of receipts, but no book. Principals were given a budget and worked within it and carried over losses and surpluses to the next year. That summer we spent every day at various stores, businesses and teachers' homes, to reissue invoices. It was backbreaking, tedious work. None of it mattered in the end. James was summoned to a formal meeting in October and fired.

"He vowed to contest his case in court. We believed that justice and the law were acquainted. We didn't believe any of it was really happening, like his cancer. We lived each day with new bombs exploding, about his case or about his life. New PET scans were taken.

We were told if the cancer had reached his brain, his life was over. For seven days we never left the house. We worked on the case and waited on the call. The cancer hadn't spread to his brain. The same day we received the court dates: November seventeenth and eighteenth. November twenty-first, he would undergo massive surgery on his lung and spleen, but he still wanted to be in court.

"Our lawyer had warned us not to lie. 'If you do, you're done.' Towards the end of the day, I saw how tired James was, and he was called. The judge asked if he knew of any other principals who had permitted such absences. James said he knew of four principals. Would he be willing to disclose the names of these individuals if he said there were to be no repercussions? There was complete silence in the court. James looked back at me.

'Your Honor, I have lost faith in an organization I worked at for twenty-seven years. I can't name the four colleagues because I don't believe they won't find themselves exactly where I find myself today.'

"Very quietly the room cleared. James was closing his briefcase when the judge approached him. All I heard was a word I couldn't make out. James smiled and nodded appreciatively. The judge shook his hand and said, 'Good luck to you.'

"The next day, a board member called in sick with a cold. Delay, now that the case seemed to have turned in James's favor. The next court day available was late March. Delay was their tactic with knowledge that James's days were running out.

"Two days later, James went through the grueling surgery that 'might' give him more time. On December twenty-first, he suffered a stroke and lost the use of his right arm. That night near midnight, after more scans, he was told he was dying. He didn't call me. 'You needed one more night's sleep.' He had at best two to three months. He wept for one day, only one. 'It's odd,' he said a month later, 'I don't ever think of the case or that surgery. I count every day we have as a gift. I'm aware of each passing hour.' I was in awe of a courage that I didn't have, of the loving man I'd never really known. One day I was gently tossing him a tennis ball to help his focus. 'I see three balls today.' 'Catch the one closest to you.' 'How come you still make me laugh?'

"James died March twelfth, 2000. I fought on for him. Five weeks after his death, he was reinstated.

"He had endured the agony of knowing, the seizures and the pain.

Yet, he never asked, 'Why me?' He wrote me notes until he couldn't. He fought for his last breath. I know I'm going on, but he's owed. I think of him with these lines from *Macbeth*. *Nothing in his life/Became him like the leaving it, He died/As one that had been studied in his death.*

"I've never stopped grieving, but back then I fell apart, had surgery, was struck from behind by a speeder who ran a red light, survived, but James's death made life seem meaningless for years, and I was often afraid. Something in me shut down. When I heard the Tibbetts were dead, I had almost forgotten that side of the battle. Their deaths didn't matter to me. Still in the aftermath of loss and self-questioning, I thought I'd had time to say our good-byes. There is never enough time. I needed one more minute to say. 'Thank you for putting up with me, James, and the life you spent with me.'"

Damiano was visibly upset.

"I'm sorry, you should have stopped me."

"I couldn't. I wanted to listen," She whispered to Matte, "I'll tell Jeff tonight."

Damiano saw Hughes to the front door. "You were both brave."

"We found ourselves in these battles before we knew what was happening."

"I know what you mean. We'll be seeing you again."

CHAPTER SEVENTEEN

DAMIANO STOOD AT the door and watched Hughes leave. In no rush to get back to the murder room, she took the stairs slowly, thinking. She found Matte already on the phone with Bell.

"We need the 2012 phone logs for this number. No, we are not looking for fraud. We have a murder investigation here." He listened. "I don't have the time for a written request, I need your supervisor." He balled his fist. "Elevator music!" Damiano sat down. "Yes, Detective Pierre Matte. Here is what we need. My badge number? Alright. In archives? Approximately, how long? This is an official request. Please put a rush on it."

"How long?"

"They have no idea. Personal calls are deleted after a year. Fraud they keep. Now, we're digging for a possible deep dive."

"I thought with computers every log was kept."

"Apparently not."

"Hughes was a cut above our usual suspects. Aside from professional interest, I liked her, but she has motive and the brains to carry out the murders."

"As soon as I saw her, I knew you would like her. I also thought you'd ask about her shoes."

"It wasn't the time."

"Let's look at what we have: Emma and Connor Tibbett, Brian and Maggie Barrett and Sandra Hughes. Five people who all have motives. Strong motives."

Damiano added, "We've read in both investigations, that the only person who had anything to do with firearms was Stu Tibbett. He went to a few firing ranges, a long time before the shooting. Black market? Who among these five would be able to access it? There is no history of the .22, because we don't have it. Without it, we're left with suppositions. If Connor or Emma, or both, conspired to get rid of the gun, it was the money, as it generally is. There was such animosity in the family that I don't think reputation was a reason. Someone managed to get the .22, and we have no proof who that was."

Pierre added, "There is no forensic evidence the bodies were moved. How did the perp get the parents sitting on the sofa so close together? Whatever pretense was employed to arrange them that way had to be done by someone they trusted. If, however, the weapon was used for that purpose, it stands to reason that one of them would have tried to make an escape. There is no sign of panic in Stu Tibbett's face. But Carol Tibbett is another story. Her face is creased, distorted."

Damiano was pressing her forehead with both hands. "If it was murder, the perp must have had the time to arrange the shot on Tibbett. According to forensics the trajectory of the bullet was very precise, perfect for a suicide. Sometimes, what appears to be true is. Then the question is why. Where did he secure the gun?"

"Toni, what if we are looking at the perfect crime?"

"There are unsolved cases, but a perfect crime?"

"Really, what's the difference?" Matte asked. "I'm asking myself, if it was Hughes, how did she get access to the house? There was no forced entry. So, why would they admit her in the first place? She must have hated Carol Tibbett. They hardly knew one another. If her pretense was a mending of wrongs, why would Tibbett, the insecure person she was, trust Hughes?"

"She could have used a disguise of some sort that would help her gain entry and departure. If she was seen, the description wouldn't expose her."

"We have to abandon suppositions because we need facts. Connor Tibbett discovered the body, but he delayed before calling 9-1-1, giving him time to conceal the weapon and later dispose of it. What does he say he was doing during that delay? I don't buy that he was in a state of shock. He hated both parents and he had access to the house," Matte thought aloud. "Take one case file home tonight and reread it. I'll take the other."

"Jeff will be angry and hurt tonight when I tell him about possible cancer."

"You're doing the right thing."

"Doesn't make it easier, or help my nerves. Jeff's solution will be a warm bath. His calmness can be so irritating. Did you remember the Ativan?"

"Yes. Stop whining. You're being brave. I mean it. You can handle Jeff."

"I'm seriously going to try to be a better person. I listened to Hughes. Fear and loss are what make us all improve, and God knows, I'm scared. Thanks for the pill." Damiano picked up her file.

CHAPTER EIGHTEEN

As Damiano drove onto the driveway, she saw that the both cars were already there, the Merc and the Jeep. There'd be no chance for a dress rehearsal. She reminded herself that the implication of cancer rested with her. She had made the best choice. The rain had stopped, but the sky was heavy, nothing like spring. Picking up the file, she let herself into the house by the garage door.

The house smelled good, lemon chicken she thought. Jeff and Luke were cutting up carrots, green beans and spinach. "I'm a lucky woman to have two good men."

Both heads turned in greeting. "Luke, put the vegetables in the pot, and we can all sit down for a while. You have work, Toni?"

"A re-read for later." Drawing in a deep breath, she began. "I have something to tell you, perhaps I should have told you earlier, but I couldn't."

"Earlier has passed, let it out. We both knew you were being secretive about something," Jeff said in a flat voice.

"Well, I had my yearly checkup."

Both men sat up, wary.

"I've had a CT scan. An oncologist appeared outside the changing room after the scan. He told me, almost apologetically, that he'd found a shadow on my right lung, perhaps scarring, or a carcinoma."

"What?" Jeff said raising his voice, "And you didn't tell me?"

"Please let me get through this."

"Go ahead," Jeff barked.

"I told the oncologist about the pleurisy and the false diagnosis of TB when I was twenty-two. I told him what he found was nothing, maybe scarring. There was also no history of cancer in our family. He wasn't impressed. He sent the results of the CT scan to my MD. Together, they said what they had seen had nothing to do with familial cancer, but there was definitely something on my lung. All my family doctor said was that I should take the PET scan. Then she appeared serious and told me to bring someone with me when she received the final results of the PET scan. That blew my nerves. It could be two weeks before she herself had the results."

Jeff had risen and gone to her.

Before he could say a word, Damiano cut in, "Let me finish. The oncologist said that if it was cancer, he'd caught it early. I went with Pierre because I needed to do this without family. I don't have the strength to comfort you or Luke. You'd scare me with your speeches and analysis. I'm scared enough as it is. Pierre was quietly present, and that's what I needed. Can you understand that?"

"I'm trying my best to understand." Jeff said quietly.

"We might have helped," Luke said gently. "Did you think of that?"

"All I had time for was fear."

"For what it's worth I'll make this short. You show none of the signs of lung cancer. I'm sure you have checked them all. You don't have to wait ten days," Jeff told her.

"We immediately checked all the signs, believe me. Why don't I have to wait for the results?"

"The hospital will have the results in five days, seven at most. Where did you go for the scan?"

"The Montreal General."

"You can go to the hospital. They hand you a copy of your results. All you need is your medical card and ten dollars. Going in from Pine Avenue, the office is straight down the hall on your right," Jeff continued.

"Mom, the two exams I have left are at night. I'll take you."

Damiano did what she hated. She broke down and cried.

Jeff put his arms around her "Know what, maybe you were right. I might have made things worse. Then again, Toni, you always do things your own way, and damned be the rest of us."

"You're right."

"Let's see what damage we can do to the chicken," Jeff offered.

"Forgive me?"

"When have I not? How are you getting some sleep with this kind of stress?"

"Two large glasses of wine."

"I'll prescribe two weeks of Ativan for you."

Matte better not open his mouth. "They would really help."

"One a night."

"Great." It was Damiano's first smile in a week and she had to hide it.

CHAPTER NINETEEN

THERE WAS ALWAYS something breaking down in the old house. This time it was the front door lock that had been sticking for a month. Along with the other things she had to do, Emma decided to stop in at ABC Locksmith located on Lagacé Avenue in Dorval, hoping that the owner Nick was not on the road. ABC was mostly a mobile service, but Nick had to be in the shop some of the time. She wanted to explain the front door problem and hoped he'd give her a good price to change the lock.

Lakeshore Road was a slower, calmer drive, and she opted for it. As she drove she remembered an incident while walking along Collins Avenue in Hollywood, Florida. some years back. Four cars were waiting at a red light, and without warning, a driver of a speeding SUV must have pressed the accelerator instead of the brake. She couldn't forget a pedestrian's shoe flying by her head. The accident happened so quickly.

When Emma noticed the car tailgating her she was thinking how dangerous it was for the driver to get that close or attempt to pass her. Before anything registered, the car started passing, sideswiping Emma and sending her car into a telephone pole installed too close to the road. She heard her own crash before she lost consciousness. The driver never stopped. Emma's car was wrapped around the pole. It didn't take long for the fire department, police and ambulance to reach the scene. With the Jaws of Life, Emma was lifted from the wreckage and transported to the Sacred Heart Hospital on Gouin Boulevard West. There her injuries were assessed: swelling in the brain that had to be relieved, a collapsed lung, a left tibia fracture and lacerations and facial bruising from the air bag.

Emma was taken immediately into surgery for a craniotomy, removal of part of the skull, relieving the pressure. Work on the lung followed, then the fracture, and finally the facial injuries. A coma was induced. When her children received the call they panicked. Michael steadied himself and called his uncle. Connor wasted no time and sped out to the West Island, collected the boys and they drove to the hospital in the Cartierville neighborhood of Montreal.

"Is Mom gonna die?" Terry, the thirteen-year-old asked, in a frightened voice.

"We won't know anything till we get there," Connor said.

"It's serious. Mom is in surgery. That's what the woman said," Michael repeated with the authority of sixteen years.

"If Mom dies, what will happen to us?"

"Shut up, Terry," Michael said, punching his brother.

They were forced to park on the street, three blocks from the hospital. They hurried to the front entrance, and were directed to the level one trauma wing. They stood in the waiting room, choosing not to sit. They were alone. "How does anyone know we're even here?" Terry wouldn't give up.

"Michael, don't shut him up. He has a point. I'll call the main desk and inform them we're here and that no one has come out to tell us anything."

Terry stuck his tongue out at his brother, something he'd never do if he were alone with him. But, Uncle Connor was there, so he went for it.

They listened while Connor spoke to the person at the desk. "At least, tell them we're here and anxious. Thank you."

"She's going to advise the unit, but we still have to wait."

"Can we get some chips?" Terry said with a sense of importance.

"NO!" three voices replied.

They waited. Connor decided to sit. The boys paced.

Connor felt like a traitor. He was distressed, but he was also relieved Emma couldn't tell anybody anything. Under pressure, she might break. He had told her too much and placed himself in jeopardy. If she died… He'd never have to worry.

Two hours later, when a doctor walked through the doors, they quickly encircled him. "We won't know definitively for another forty-eight hours." He explained what procedures had been performed. "She's hanging in, and that's a good sign."

"She's a fighter," Terry said proudly.

"Should we wait?" Connor asked.

"That's entirely up to you," the doctor replied.

"Will you give us reports?"

"We will."

"We'll wait. We can sleep in chairs."

"There's a cafeteria," the doctor said.

"Good, we are all set," Connor said. He was the boss. "Michael, here's some money. Find the cafeteria and buy sandwiches and coffee and milk. Do you have your father's number?"

"On my phone."

"Give it to me, and I'll call him while you're buying the food."

Terry and Bobby sat and watched. Connor left the room to make the call to Devon and relayed what had occurred.

"But at the moment, Em's okay?"

"Hanging in, the doctor said. I'll stay the night, but they're your kids."

"I know that. I'll see you guys at nine tomorrow and take over from there."

"Good, because I have Zoom meetings tomorrow. I can't miss the meetings because I called them."

At three-fifteen, the kids were asleep, a different doctor, a surgeon, entered the waiting area. "The surgery went well without problems. The lung has been taken care of. We'll deal with the fracture today. The lacerations have been cleaned. Now we wait."

"What does a craniotomy entail?" Connor asked.

"Healing time is four to eight weeks. The incisions cause a soreness for a week, we watch the swelling and remind the patient that rest and careful head movements are essential. But each patient is different, so what I've given you are generalities."

"How long will my sister be in the hospital?"

"The swelling and its decrease will determine – a couple of weeks. She'll need home care too."

Connor felt a stab of guilt. He wanted Emma to recover. She was his only family. But he couldn't sleep that night because Emma was also a threat to him as long as she was alive.

CHAPTER TWENTY

DEVON WAS TRUE TO his word and he knew enough to ask where he might pick up Emma's personal things. They would bring fresh clothes the day she was released. He checked her purse to see if the three thousand he'd given her was there. He hadn't expected it to be. Emma had probably stuck the money in her modest jewelry box in a compartment under the jewelry. Connor told Michael to go home with Devon and help with his brothers. He would stay at the hospital with his sister.

No one spoke on the way home. Devon rarely saw them, and there were awkward moments. When they reached the house on Broadview, as expected it was neat as a pin. Devon recalled that his wife was a clean freak. As they went through the door, Devon said, "Boys, we haven't been on the best of terms. But now we're stuck together."

"Doesn't mean we have to talk," Bobby grumbled.

"True, but if we don't work out, there is always foster care. Stay down here. I have to check on something." Emma's bedroom was the first at the top of the stairs. The small compartment at the bottom of the jewel box was empty. He knew Emma wouldn't have deposited the money in the bank because she needed to spend some of it the following week. He hated confrontations – mostly he ran from them. For the first time, he wanted to do right by Emma. "Let's sit in the kitchen." He waited till the boys were seated before he spoke. "I gave your mother three thousand in back child support, and I think that one of you has taken the money. It's not where it should be. I've done some shitty things in my life, but this theft is right up there."

"You're a lousy father and a cheat." Michael snarled.

"Both true, but I'm trying to change. I want the money on the kitchen table in two hours. A portion of it was for your senior prom, Michael, and there was some for your birthday, Bobby. I don't care who took the money. I just want it back. Look, I'll even walk around the block, so I won't know who took it. Are you listening?"

Nobody answered, but Terry looked like he was about to cry. He began pulling bills out of his jeans pocket. "I swear I didn't know it was that much, and it was too late to put it back." He deposited the crumpled pile on the table.

"Know what, Terry, it takes courage to own up and not sneak the money back so no one would ever know. That's something to be proud of."

"He's still a thief," Bobby scoffed.

"How about we pick up pizza for lunch?"

"Okay!"

"Are you up to going to school this afternoon?"

Michael shot back. "I want to stay home and hear how Mom is. I'm also fried. We're all fried."

"I'll call the ICU in an hour," Devon said, as he headed up to the bathroom, taking two stairs at a time. The foul odor assaulted his nostrils at the first bedroom. "What the hell is this stench?" He shouted over the banister.

Terry laughed hard, straining his throat. "Our bedrooms."

When Devon returned, he found the boys in the kitchen, waiting on the pizza as promised. "Does your mother have strong garbage bags?"

"In the garage," Terry answered.

"All right, Terry, get out there and bring back three."

Bobby and Michael sensed trouble and slouched on the chairs. Terry dragged in the bags.

"I thought we'd have an early breakfast/lunch, but the pigsties I found upstairs disgusted me. The rest of the house is clean."

"Mom says she'll cook for us and wash our clothes, but she won't touch our rooms. We don't mind the mess."

"Guys, your mom's in critical condition. If she survives, the least you can do is clean up the pile of trash I saw upstairs. Each of you take a bag, you have one hour. Put the dirty clothes in the bathroom hamper, the rotting food and garbage in the bags. One hour!"

"That's not enough time. It took us a year to mess up the room."

"Two large all dressed pizzas will be here in an hour. If they get cold, I'll toss them. Do you guys understand? I'll inspect the rooms first and then order the food."

"That's blackmail!"

"Whatever works."

The boys grabbed a bag and rocketed up the stairs. For the next hour, all Devon heard was noise, no swearing, but boy noise. He switched on the radio to CJAD at the top of the hour for news of the accident. He preferred CBC, but he didn't want to make changes. They did not identify the victim, except to say she was a woman in her late thirties or perhaps early forties in critical condition at the Sacred Heart Hospital. Devon noted the anchor had used the French name. The stolen vehicle had been abandoned in Lachine. The police had no suspects. There had been no reported burglaries in the area, so police suspected a joy ride gone wrong. Witnesses were asked to call police with much needed information to the provided number. Devon stood wringing his hands, hoping the accident was unintentional. The only person he thought who might want to silence Emma was Connor because she had been frightened that afternoon. He read that lingering fear when they had dinner.

He called the hospital to learn Emma had passed an 'uneventful' night. That was good news he was told. The swelling had receded. Could her boys see her? One minute each, he was told. He called for the pizza.

The full garbage bags were dragged bumping down the stairs and dumped in the garage. Devon was shocked to see spotless rooms that reeked of Febreze. "We'll tackle the wash tonight." The pizzas were devoured in minutes. All Devon got was one slice and crust that Terry didn't like. "First, we shower. Then we'll drive back to the hospital. You can see your mother for a minute. What's that on the counter?"

"Mom's agenda, but it's locked. None of us can find the key."

"So, you've looked?"

"Way back, but we came up with nothing. A few nights ago, Mom was crying and writing in the agenda. She closed it when she saw me. She must have forgotten to take it upstairs with her."

CHAPTER TWENTY-ONE

FOR THE NEXT FEW HOURS, Connor had one-minute visits with Emma. Why had he confided in her? He feared his own sister. He looked down at her swollen face, the cuts red and raw, and, for a few moments, he wished she had died. His secrets would be safe, and he could fabricate a story about his father and Emma. He'd be the only source. The next time he stared down at Emma, he felt a grudging bond with her. He was alone now, he wasn't twenty anymore, and she was his only family.

The agenda struck him like a bolt of lightning. Even if she died, the damned book was in the house. Why was Emma keeping a diary like a young girl? He had no doubt she'd written every damning word he shared. What he needed was the book found and destroyed. As he was leaving the ICU, he noticed the police questioning one of the physicians. He'd be suspected further if he didn't reveal who his sister was. The cops were uniforms, not detectives. If he withheld that information, and they learned of it later, their suspicion of him would heighten.

He approached the uniform who wasn't talking. "May I speak to you about the hit-and-run?"

He had the cop's attention. "Detectives Toni Damiano and Pierre Matte of Major Crimes have reopened the case of my parents' murder/suicide."

"That ten-year-old case?"

"That one. I am Connor Tibbett and the victim of the hit-and-run is my sister Emma Tibbett. They would want to be informed."

"Don't move." The uniform took out his phone and called Major Crimes. "I'll wait." Within seconds, "Detective Matte? Good." His recounting was succinct. "I see. Will do, Detective." He turned to Connor. "They're both coming out and they want you here."

"I have to grab a sandwich. I haven't eaten since yesterday."

"Food will have to wait. You can't be MIA when Major Crimes gets here."

"What is this? Am I under arrest?"

"No, I want those detectives to find you here. Their orders."

Connor wanted to take off, but waited instead. He was tired, sticky and could smell his own breath. Damiano and Matte arrived in record time. Connor was nodding off when the detectives walked into the room. He shot up, rubbing both eyes.

"How is your sister doing?" Damiano asked.

"As well as anyone on a ventilator, in an induced coma, with part of her skull open to reduce swelling of her brain, can be. They were able to fix the collapsed lung. I see her for a minute every hour, I've cheated twice, sneaking in when the nurse didn't see me."

Matte asked matter-of-factly, "Where were you…"

"Jesus, she's my sister. I was Zooming and I can give you my clients' names."

"That would be helpful. There were skid marks but nothing to suggest your sister was purposely run off the road," Matte added.

"Then, why bother…"

"Protocol."

The boys and Devon rushed into the room. "How's Mom?" Michael asked for all three boys.

"She's holding on. The nurse will walk each of you in. Your mom looks bad, but remember she hasn't given up. You can't either." Connor had his hands on Terry's shoulders.

The boys who walked out of the ICU were visibly frightened and weeping, except for Michael who was doing his best to be strong. Not one of them said anything. They huddled together. Devon was the last to see Emma. His devastation and worry were obvious.

"How long are you going to stay, Connor?"

"I'll go home now and shower, change clothes, postpone appointments and get back here in ninety minutes or so. During the first forty-eight hours, I don't want Emma to be alone."

Michael spoke, "We'll stay until you get back. Then we're going to clean up the mess in the basement for Mom. What about you?" he asked looking at Devon.

"I'll stay with you guys."

The boys were glad of that, but tried their best not to show Devon.

"Is Mom going to die? I didn't mean to take the money!"

"Just shut up," Bobby hissed. "Don't make things worse."

"What money?" Connor wanted to know.

"Child support that was misplaced," Devon said.

Connor saw Damiano and Matte standing by, but listening intently. "I'm still free to go?" Connor said bluntly.

"You still are. We have to consider all possibilities," Damiano replied. Matte and Damiano wanted to be sure Tibbett was not involved in the accident.

"To me that suggests you have made no progress."

"We are not a forty-minute episode on Netflix. Someone has to have seen the driver of the other vehicle. It's a matter of time." Damiano noticed that Matte had taken a call and walked away from the family for privacy.

His call ended before she reached him. "We have info on Hughes's phone logs, and I have more questions for her. We can leave. We can't interview Emma Tibbett. I don't think we have any worries about either man disappearing." They left quietly. Damiano drove and Matte called Hughes asking her to come to the division.

"I'm in a class right now, but I could leave if it's important."

"It is."

"I'm glad I chose to work in water colors. The cleanup is so much easier. Give me an hour."

CHAPTER TWENTY-TWO

As soon as Damiano and Matte were back at the division, they went straight to the research office. Marie Doucette had been working the phone logs, locating numbers, with particular attention to any calls around the time of the crimes and after. They picked up her notes and headed back downstairs to the boardroom. Matte began to read. "The first calls were to Florida, specifically, Sunny Isles. The second to Toronto, and the last call was local."

"Did Marie match them with names?"

"She did."

"Spill them, then."

"The Florida calls were to a condo manager, one Michel Benoit." Matte laughed. "Seems like every French Quebecer vacations in Florida, and some stay months working there, like this Benoit. Hughes probably rented a condo from him."

Damiano quickly cut in and added. "I'm thinking of how easy it would be to secure a gun without filing papers. I wonder if she always flew, or drove to have a car there for the vacation. It would be easy to smuggle a gun across the border. If she is a longtime renter or owner, it would be even simpler. She'd know people. We'd have a premeditated crime."

"Save those thoughts. I better meet her at the door." Matte wasn't expecting to meet Hughes in white painters' jeans with a French blue and white shirt, toting a jacket on one shoulder.

"It would have taken me too long to change. This casual look takes just as much time as the ordinary clothes. The jeans were clean this morning," she smiled easily.

"Actually, I quite like the look."

"Truth, so do I." As they walked down the corridor, she thought the long walk was unnerving.

Entering the large boardroom, she acknowledged Damiano and asked, "Well, where do we start?"

"We'll begin with your phone calls the night of the murders." Damiano read out the first number.

"My sister and best friend lives in TO. We often talk twice a day."

Then, Damiano read out the Florida number.

"James and I rented an ocean-side condo for years, and I continued renting after James died. Each year, I retraced our steps and remembered our times there. My sister came once with me. Then my best friend took her place. I'd rent for a month, Kathy had only two weeks."

"Fly or drive?"

"Drove twice and then flew the rest of the time."

"Have you ever held a gun?"

"Never, and I wouldn't want to. You are no doubt thinking how easy it would be to get a gun in Florida. There are a few young Cuban families, an older New York couple and the rest of us are from Quebec, including the condo manager. I don't know of anyone who'd know where to buy one. Most of the time, we feel that we've never left our province. We all do feel the place is as safe as home."

Matte read the last number.

"A good friend who stays up late."

Damiano began in her serious tone. "The Tibbetts were murdered or died between eight and ten. You have no alibi for the time."

"I am going to try to piece together what Netflix film I might have been watching. As I said, their identities were not disclosed for a couple of days. While we West Islanders worried about a possible murderer hiding somewhere, we were busy locking doors. We thought it might be teenagers pulling off a robbery that went terribly wrong."

"I don't know now who'd remember that my car never left the garage the night of the murders. People move. Ten years is too long to recall such a thing. I'm a suspect then?"

"Yes, you are," Damiano answered. "But if you come up with something that clears you, let us know."

"I want to add a thought," Hughes said gravely. "I hope in your lifetime you are not judged by someone who doesn't know you and is in possession of exaggerated lies about you. And worse, believes them. If Tibbett's letters had ended up with my principal, they would have been torn up as was her second letter assault on a colleague. James wasn't lucky, not in this predicament or with his cancer. Fate was cruel and merciless. He handled both with dignity and grace."

Matte walked Hughes to the front door and re-joined Damiano. "I know exactly what you're thinking."

"Which is?"

"If it walks like a duck and talks like a duck. Maybe it is a murder/suicide. Hughes is an intelligent woman who may be deceiving us with her straightforward answers, but maybe that's exactly what they are, straightforward. It's the bloody .22 that muddies the whole case."

"Was the gun disposed of to get the insurance money or did the murderer take it? The gun is our answer, but I don't think we will ever find it."

Matte couldn't let go. "Connor Tibbett is a definite suspect. Due to circumstances, we leave him be for now. Let's question the dentists, Brian and Maggie."

"I'll make the call right now. We can't afford to lose time."

CHAPTER TWENTY-THREE

DEVON SAT ALONE after seeing Emma. One by one, the boys slowly crept over to him. Terry's heart was beating with one question. "You think Mom will dic, don't you?"

"I don't know, but she's hurt really bad. Don't cry, Terry. Tears don't help, stay strong for her." He signaled for Michael and Bobby to join them. "When you see your Mom today, touch her hand, so she'll know she's not alone."

"How do you know that?" Michael challenged.

"Those facts have been published before, more than once."

"I believe that," Bobby said. "You gotta believe something, right?"

"I agree," Devon concurred. Time passed quickly, and when Connor rushed down the hall and into the waiting room, it seemed he'd just left.

"How is she?"

"We haven't seen any doctors, but we've seen Emma. She's a fighter, I hope," Devon said, uncertainly.

"I am going to demand to see a doctor. You guys can go home. What arrangements are you making for the boys, Devon?"

"We'll settle that when we get home, but I have to work tonight. We can arrange something. Either way, I'll let you know, or Michael will." They left Connor with Emma. "Let's hit that wash as soon as we're home." Michael was a master washer.

"Separate the darks into one pile, the whites into another. Bobby, get the pods. Let's go. We're looking at five washes."

As soon as the sorting was done, and the piles lay across the basement table, Devon asked the boys to come upstairs. "Here's how I see things. I work casino security from seven till three. I go home and crash. At three-thirty in the afternoon, I'll be outside St. Thomas High School and we'll go back to the hospital. Michael, have you made dinner before?"

"Yeah, but I hate cooking."

"What can you make tonight? We have to work as a team."

"Bullshit."

"That and more, I've let your mom down so often, I want her to know that we all care for her for once."

"Beans and hot dogs."

"What?"

"I can make those."

"Good, but the dishes have to be washed and dried."

"I cook, so they clean up."

"Before I leave, I have to tell you all something that we keep to ourselves, understood?"

"About Uncle Connor?"

"NO. NO. Can you keep this secret?"

"I want to hear it," Michael was adamant.

"You know the police are re-opening the murder/suicide of your grandparents."

"They couldn't solve it in two tries, so they won't solve it now," Michael said.

"The detectives are digging deep, Emma told me. When we met for dinner, she was really scared of them, and she saw Connor too, and she was just as frightened of him. I advised her to say nothing to the detectives because they can twist words around. They warned her of prison. She may have written nothing about all this in her agenda, but she might have done the opposite. Those are her private thoughts that she never meant to share. That's why the book is locked. With your permission, I want to take it and hide it. Connor may worry that he said too much to her and she got it in that agenda of hers. The agenda is Emma's and no one has the right to read it. I'll keep it safe and unopened until she herself asks for it.

"I trusted you to return the money – I need you to trust that I have your mother's best interests at heart. I'll also leave the money here. You can each take a tenner to spend. The rest goes into the dish cupboard, first shelf."

"What do we say if Uncle Connor remembers Mom's agenda and asks to see it? He knows about it."

"Tell him you haven't seen it in a while. Maybe Mom threw it out. You don't know or care. I need each of you to protect your mom's privacy."

"That's a lie!" Bobby blurted out.

"To keep your mom safe. One real fact, the truth is overrated."

"Are you our dad again?"

"I always was. I know your mom called me the ghost. But I'm here now."

Before the boys had left the hospital, Connor went to the nurses' station and demanded to see a doctor. "No one has told us anything in a day and a half." The nurse told Connor how busy the trauma floor was, but she got on the phone. "The doctor will meet with you in the patient's room."

Emma seemed to tense up when Connor sat down beside her. Was he imagining it, or was Emma reacting to his presence? It took about an hour before a surgeon in green scrubs walked into the room.

Connor was grateful he was fluent in English. Connor was comfortable in French, but not with medical terminology. "The surgery went well. The bone flap we removed has been replaced and we are bringing the patient out of the induced coma. While we can control the pain, the patient still feels some of it. There will be scarring, and pain around the wound, as well as shooting pain in the face and numbness. It will be more acute during the next four to seven days. I expect her to make a decent recovery. Her health is good and she is strong. Because your sister is part of the health care family practice, we were able to arrange a suite for her at Le Vivalis on the West Island. They have a rehab floor there, but first she will stay with us for another few days."

"Thank you. If anything untoward occurs, I hope we will be notified."

"Certainly."

"Can my sister hear me if I whisper?"

"I can't say for certain. Each patient is different." He was up on his feet and left the ICU.

Connor had to leave the room as well. Pacing and questioning, his steps were stiff and deliberate. She could not have told Devon anything, or he would have read the animosity in Devon and it wasn't there. Emma couldn't have been so stupid as to have written in that bloody diary or whatever she called the thing. She'd keep the house she loved by shutting her mouth. Just the same, he'd find that damn book and see for himself. What he had told her was strong evidence of what, of murder. That his father was still alive when he got home, and he waited until he was dead to call for help. Connor needed time to be alone with the boys who must know the whereabouts of the damned book. He didn't want Devon involved until the book was in his hands.

CHAPTER TWENTY-FOUR

DAMIANO WAS PREPARING to call the Barretts' clinic when her phone rang. "Lieutenant Detective Damiano. Major Crimes." She listened for only seconds before she asked the caller, "Would you repeat that again? I'm putting you on speaker."

"Police Poste de Quartier 5, Constable Jean-Paul Bouchard speaking."

"This might not be of concern to you, but there was a collision on Lakeshore Road. The name of the victim is Emma Tibbett."

"Detective Matte and I know about the incident, Constable, we're working on a cold case, the murder/suicide of Ms. Tibbett's parents."

"I read about it, and I caught the name today."

"Go on."

"A half-hour ago, the driver responsible for the collision on Lakeshore Road came to the station with his father. He is a fourteen-year-old boy who apparently spotted the car keys to his neighbor's vehicle hanging in the garage when he was hired to mow their lawn while they were with their daughter in Toronto. He swears he wasn't speeding on Lakeshore Road, but he tried to pass a woman who was driving very slowly. He didn't notice the curve in the road. Only when he was passing the car, did he notice the oncoming vehicle and panicked. He didn't figure he had time to pull back behind her so he forced the woman's car onto the sidewalk to avoid a head-on collision. He didn't realize how badly he'd sideswiped her vehicle. Abandoning the car in a panic, he fled the scene. Today, he confessed to his father who immediately brought him to the station. The victim was a stranger to him. This was his first time behind the wheel. His father was furious, telling the boy he had just ruined his whole life and nearly killed a woman with three children who attended his own school, St. Thomas High School. The boy said he never meant to hurt anyone, and in my opinion, he is still in shock."

"The day of the accident, we called in a reconstructionist, Detective Constable Panet, and her team, to the scene. While they found no evidence of excess speed, the young driver of the Toyota Camry was clearly at fault. The head injuries incurred by the victim indicate her vehicle was struck from the side. The boy was not belted and the victim was. Her facial abrasions were caused by the exploding air bag.

"We can handle this charge of driving dangerously, causing bodily harm. Let's keep in touch to exchange further information. The boy will be sent to the youth criminal system. Do you wish to question him? We can delay the process."

"Not for the present. You're certain there is no connection to the victim?"

"Yes."

"Please keep me posted with any new information."

"*Tout à fait.*"

After the call, Damiano confirmed with Matte that they didn't need to speak to the boy.

"No, he's responsible for injuring Emma, but he appears to have no direct connection to our case."

Before Damiano attempted to make the Barrett call again, she said to Matte, "We already figured that the weapon he handed us wouldn't be a match. The whole case rests on the missing gun. Here's another dead end. Barrett already knew that."

"Sure he did."

"Doctor Barrett, Detective Damiano. I need you in for further questioning. Have you sought legal assistance?"

"Not as of yet. I have other issues I'm dealing with. I am willing to be questioned without counsel. I have nothing to hide. When do you want to see me?"

"Is today possible?"

"Four-ish?"

"We'll see you then."

Matte noticed that Damiano looked worried.

"Stop thinking about the scan results. You'll drive yourself crazy."

"You do know that cancer at our age is at its most aggressive. Chemo and immunotherapy will be much less effective."

"You don't even know if you have cancer, Toni. Can you not wait three and a half more days? I have never known you to back away from a fight."

"It's a fight on my own terms."

"Just dying, surrendering?"

"Let's change the subject, Pierre."

"The crime, cold, calculated, neat, precise, almost perfect – doesn't that hint at either of our dentists?" Matte said in his detailed mode.

"Twelve years after their son's drowning, at a time when they are both well established? Let's eat something. I couldn't manage breakfast."

"You seem a little drugged the last two mornings. Maybe you should switch to half an Ativan."

"It's my nerves – they're locked."

"I brought two tuna sandwiches. Have one. I'll get them from my locker."

"God, thanks. I'll look after the coffee."

As soon as the food arrived, Damiano grabbed a sandwich and went to work on it.

"Slow down. Why do you always eat as though you haven't eaten in a week? I put bits of celery, parsley, onion and green olives in that sandwich."

"Oh alright." Damiano stopped and chewed. "It's very good for tuna."

"You're welcome."

They both cleaned up and walked downstairs. Damiano and Matte walked to the boardroom.

A constable called to say a Doctor Barrett had arrived, and he led the doctor to the boardroom.

"You're early, Doctor."

"I finished early and I hate wasting time."

"Have a seat across from us, please," Matte directed him.

"I can't believe I'm even a suspect."

"Back then, along with your grief, were you angry?"

"At whom?"

"At your wife and the Tibbetts?"

He rubbed the bridge of his nose and his mouth. "I suppose."

"Were you ever able to forgive your wife? I know you've told us how Piper, is it? escaped your attention once. We both have read that parents never fully recover. Is that true for you?" Damiano sat back on her chair to wait for the reply.

"I lost my little brother to leukemia. He was four, so Calvin's birth was that much more precious to me. I'm not a perfect man, so I could never forgive either one. Maggie was so fragile that I couldn't attack her. But she saw the anger in me every day. I said once, 'You were on your cell. Why didn't you walk back to Calvin? He'd be alive if you had!' She broke down and stayed broken through ten years of therapy."

"What about the Tibbetts?"

"I saw them in Chapters one day. I walked up behind them and spat on him, not to his face, on his back. I didn't want a lawsuit. That's the extent of my attack and bravery."

"You still sound angry, Doctor," Matte cut in.

"You're bringing back horrible memories that have never really left. To be a killer, I think one needs to be brave."

"Actually, all one needs is anger, Doctor," Damiano smiled. With that comment, the detectives ended the session and stopped recording.

"We're no further ahead," Matte showed some of his exasperation.

CHAPTER TWENTY-FIVE

CONNOR CALLED THE BOYS just before nine. Michael picked up because he was the boss now and, besides, Bobby and Terry had showered again and gone to bed without any prompting. "Is Mom alright?"

"So far. She hasn't regained consciousness, but the doctor said every patient is different. I'm placing ice chips on her lips so they don't dry up. How are you guys?"

"Fine. Dad left for work at the casino. He works high security, kinda cool. He'll be back by three tomorrow to take us to the hospital."

Connor wanted to add, *that's where he wants to be.* Instead, he said, "No problems with him then?"

"He said he wants to change. I believe him."

"I hope he means it this time. I'm staying till they kick me out." It was not the right time to mention the agenda. He needed to be in the house, preferably alone.

Michael was beside the phone when it rang again. He thought it was Uncle Connor. "We're fine. What? Luke?"

"So, it was your mom in the accident? When you all weren't in school, we figured it out. Tough."

"Yeah."

"Is she going to be okay?"

"It's serious, man. I don't know."

"I know who the driver is."

"What?"

"The driver."

"You freakin' sure?"

"All the guys figured it out. A fourteen-year-old kid who's absent. I swear, we know!"

"Who is it?"

"A kid named Andrew Anderson in grade nine at St. Thomas. He's probably being held by the cops. We added up the parts. Matt called his house. The father hung up on us. That's when we really knew."

"Shit!"

"I have his address and phone number. Do you want them? Want help?"

"Give me the address."

"St. Louis Boulevard, number 176. I'm willing to help you, Mike. You need a lookout."

"I gotta think."

"About what? I heard that your mother could die. You can't be a pussy about this, Mike."

"We have enough trouble as it is. My mom wouldn't want me to get into more."

"Who's with you right now?"

"No one. My brothers are in bed."

"It's perfect then! We both sneak out, I stand watch, and you do what you have to do. With me as your lookout, we don't get caught. We're back home before anyone knows we ever left. The kid's a juvenile, so he'll get off easily. Your mom won't be so lucky."

"If I do anything, I do it alone. The cops can't make you cough up what you don't know."

"Damn, I'd never give you up. Never! You need someone checking the street and the houses. You work alone, you're asking for trouble."

"Let me think."

"We could use our bikes, hide both and then hightail it."

"Luke, two kids racing off on bikes? We'd be spotted. If we go, we go on foot. Wear dark clothes and grab a hoodie."

"We're doing it?"

"Andrew should know what it feels like to be sideswiped."

"When?"

"How soon can you get here?"

"Max, fifteen minutes."

"I'll be waiting outside."

By the time the boys hit St. Louis Boulevard, they were wet and cold from the drizzle. "The house must be halfway down the street. At least we're on the right side, Luke. Catch your breath, we run slowly, you stand guard, give me the clear signal, and I throw the half brick."

Two minutes later, they saw their target. "Through the front window?"

"Where else?"

"Jesus, what if you hit someone, Mike?"

"Now you worry."

"It's a small house."

"Maybe we should forget this."

But Mike didn't. Without warning, Michael launched the brick. It crashed right through a large square window in the front of the house. A woman screamed. The boys tore down the street. Luke soon turned right and disappeared. On his way rushing home Michael slipped on a patch of ice and fell hard against the curb. Smothering a yelp of pain, he rose and limped the rest of way to the house. He went down to the basement, stripped, and threw his wet clothes into the washer and turned it on. Thankful for the basement shower, he sprayed ice cold water on his knee before he toweled off. He called Luke's cell. "Swear!"

"On my life."

CHAPTER TWENTY-SIX

SUE ANDERSON WAS AT the sink, cleaning up a late dinner of Rob's special hamburgers. She let out a scream as the brick crashed through the front window, sending two of Rob's hand-carved wooden ducks careening across the narrow room. Rob was in the shower, but he heard the noise. He ran out with just a towel wrapped around his waist. "What the...?" He saw the brick lying on the floor and sized up the situation immediately. Returning to the bedroom, he stepped into his jeans, yanked on a sweater and grabbed his jacket.

"Boots?" Sue asked. "Whoever did this are long gone, Rob."

He rushed out the door anyway and automatically turned right, then left. There were no cars on the road or bikes. "Shit! Kids!" He ran down Broadview and doubled over a few blocks down, wheezing and aching. "Damn knees! They all know it was Andrew." He stood, wiped the spittle from his mouth and went back. He hated dealing with cops, bad memories from his pot-smoking days back when it was illegal. "Now, we'll probably need protection. I'll call the cops and the insurance." He thought of all the damage the kids could do to the house he had remodeled himself over the last twenty years. He had built the separate garage outside. Some part of him was everywhere, even the front steps and stained door. By the time he was back home, he was angry. "That son of ours!"

Sue had the insurance papers as he walked in and took off his boots. "I'm looking up the police number."

"I thought you'd know it."

"You thought right." Rob made both calls and they sat and waited. "I'm glad you didn't clean up. The cops have to see this. That brick could have hit either one of us."

"We're lucky then."

"Oh yeah, real lucky. If the poor woman dies or is injured for life..."

"We might have to move."

"Nobody is going to force me from my own house. I've worked since I was seventeen. You've worked hard too. What got into Andrew?"

"He wasn't thinking, and you know he never meant to hurt anyone."

"Didn't mean to hurt anyone, means fuck all! Doesn't change anything."

"You were no angel, Rob."

"Yeah, I know. But Andrew is a good kid. What got into his head?"

"Cars!"

Exactly seventeen minutes later, the police parked in front of the house. The doorbell that Rob had installed last year rang. Two officers entered together. They bent down to take off their boots.

"Never mind, officers. We have to clean up anyway."

The wooden floors in the living room creaked as the officers walked inside. They bagged the brick. One officer spoke, "You were lucky not to have been struck. Do you have any idea of who might have done this?"

"Yes," Rob said before the officer could finish. He filled them in. "Well, I too, think it's kids. I will ask to have a car close by for a few days."

"What happens then? We're on our own?"

The lead officer thought and spoke. "We'll pay a visit to the family and the school with warnings to both. That usually ends it, sir. You have insurance?"

"Yes."

"Good, everything costs more now. I'll fill out a report. When did this occur?"

"An hour ago."

"And you saw no one?"

"I ran down St. Louis and didn't see a soul. I was in the shower, so they had a head start."

"And a few years," an officer smiled.

"Time was…"

"Me too. Well, good luck to you. I'll send you a copy of the report for your insurance. I need your email."

After they left, Sue called the insurance company. "I was thinking as you spoke, what if that mother dies, like you said. How long are they keeping Andrew do you know?"

"Until his hearing because of the severity of the injury."

"Can I see him?"

"I'll call and ask. I'm sure you can and I'll drive. I know your nerves are shot."

"And yours?"

"That's why it's better if we go together in the morning."

"Poor Andrew."

CHAPTER TWENTY-SEVEN

MICHAEL LAY ON HIS BED while his knee throbbed no matter how hard he rubbed it. He limped downstairs and put his clothes in the dryer and stayed there, slumped over. The knee wasn't broken, but he wasn't able to walk without a visible limp. A thought crept over any sense of righteous revenge. What if the brick had struck someone? What if… He cut that thought, but the thought had claws. He'd go to juvenile. Who'd take care of Terry and Bobby? Devon had been good to them, but that never lasted. As his mom said, as soon as he lost, Devon would disappear, and she was left on her own. Well, Mom couldn't help now, and, if he was arrested, what then. He made the decision as soon as his jeans were dry.

He got dressed, pulled on his jacket that was still wet and tied his boots this time. He slowly limped back to St. Louis Boulevard. When he noticed the cop car he ducked awkwardly behind the side of a house. The patrol car passed. Michael realized he had to make it to the Anderson house before the cop made another pass by the house. He didn't feel the tears streaking down his face as he forced his knee to run. He pounded on the front door. It was well after three in the morning.

Rob hadn't gone to bed. He sat stern-faced with a beer in his hand, ready for another assault and not too sober. His fists had never let him down and he balled his right fist as he walked unsteadily to the door. He'd missed a few slivers of glass he saw. He opened the door, ready to strike.

Michael burst into the room right past Rob.

"What the …?"

Sue had run out in her nightgown. "Rob?"

No one could stop Michael. "I threw the brick. My name is Michael Tibbett. My mother is in a coma – she might die, she might die. I'm in charge of my younger brothers. My parents are divorced. I felt I had to do something to make up for what happened to her." He shouted even louder, "My mother might die!" He dropped to the floor, hugging his knee. "Please don't call the cops on me. I have money to pay for the window. Here is six hundred dollars! It's money for my prom and back child support from my father. If you need more money, I can make it and I promise to pay you. Please don't send me to jail. What will happen to my brothers? If my mom survives, she'll need my help. We don't have money for extra help. I am so sorry – I have never done anything like this in my life."

"You could have killed my wife!" Rob hollered. "You might have blinded me. You little fool!" He checked his Rickenbacker 350v63 hanging on the wall. "Do you know how much that guitar is worth, you little shit? John Lennon used that guitar on the Ed Sullivan Show."

Michael didn't hear anything about the guitar because he had already dissolved into tears. "I know it's really bad," he whimpered.

"What is it you know?"

"I could have killed someone," he said louder. "I haven't slept in two days. No one cares about my mother as much as her kids. I have to pretend to Bobby and Terry that Mom will be okay. But I don't know. I don't know anything. I am so sorry."

Rob was short but strong and muscled from tough labor and tougher sports. "Get up off your knees." The fact that Michael was taller made no difference. Rob could easily have taken the kid out, but Sue gave him the eye.

"Our Andrew didn't mean to hurt your mother. The police told us he wasn't speeding. But he shouldn't have been driving. You're lucky Rob and I were not hurt."

"I wish we could change everything," Michael said.

"You're not alone. Our deductible is five hundred dollars. Right, Rob?"

"You're not just going to let the kid go, without charges, Sue?"

"Yes, we are. We're not hurt. The boy is needed at home."

"You are one lucky son of a bitch that I have the best wife in the world."

Michael didn't know what to say. He handed over the six hundred. "Keep it all, Mrs. Anderson. I'll never be able to thank you enough."

Sue returned one hundred dollars.

"You can't walk home on that knee. You may have torn the meniscus."

"It's okay, sir."

"Go outside, and, if you can, hop into my truck." As they left, Rob poked his head back inside. "I'll settle with you later." He didn't manage a smile, but Sue did.

No one spoke in the truck until they reached the house on Broadview. "Remember that you got away easy with us not pressing charges. My son is a good boy, but…"

"I understand. Thank you, sir."

"Take care of the knee."

As soon as he quietly opened the door, Michael called Luke.

"Dammit! I was asleep."

"I went back to the house and confessed and…"

"What the hell!"

"I never gave you up. I handed them five hundred bucks to cover the deductible and they are not pressing charges."

"There goes your prom."

"Yeah, but…"

"You're lucky."

"I know it. Do you still have the crutches you needed last year?"

"Yeah."

"I fucked up my knee, so I need them."

"I'll meet you at your place tomorrow with the crutches. They can be adjusted, you know."

"Thanks. They'll do for now. Think I'll need an X-ray."

"Shit!"

"And a story."

"Ah, you missed the bottom stair. Did that, really knocked both knees."

"Right." Michael hung up and rolled his shoulders, and they ached too.

CHAPTER TWENTY-EIGHT

THE NEXT MORNING DAMIANO found Matte on the phone in the murder room, raising a hand indicating he needed to be alone. That was fine with her, she had calls to make. Her skin was as tight as a drum. Closing the blinds to her glass office, Damiano tried stretching, swinging her arms in pinwheels and added bends. Nothing helped, Ativan as well. One had to be somewhat relaxed for the pill to work. Damiano wasn't so sure of her brave stance. Her bold statement of living out her life with no chemo or radiation was a tough gesture, a 'no' to what was coming into her life. The reality of meeting her death head on, very different. She shivered before tapping in one of her two calls. So far, she learned only that Doctor Maggie Barrett was good at her work and very private. She was not expecting this call to be any different.

Mary Blake took the call after five rings, just before the call went to voice mail. Damiano introduced herself. "Maggie Barrett? We went to high school together, and I was a bridesmaid at her wedding. Close as thieves, we once were."

"Once?"

"After Calvin drowned, Maggie cut herself off from everyone. Pretty normal – I would have done the same. The sad eventuality is that after Piper was born, nothing changed. The therapy she had begun continued for years. The few attempts I made to renew our friendship were gently rebuffed. First it was 'I can't breathe in this house.' Years later, 'my therapist maintains I will better heal by leaving the past and starting afresh.' That's exactly what Maggie did."

"You had no contact since?"

"About a year ago, Maggie called. We had lunch; but it never went past that. There was too much scar tissue on both sides. We are different people. I guess I was hurt at being put aside though I understood it. I wanted to help, but Maggie said I reminded her that Calvin was dead. I didn't forgive *her* because I thought best buds were forever. It's a sad end to a life-long friendship. Maggie was a great mother – she was that."

Damiano thought again of the two friendships she had laid waste in her career. "Thank you for your time."

"You're welcome. I know enough not to ask what this call concerns."

"Have a good day."

Damiano was on the verge of a breakdown. Matte had opened her door quietly. "Don't."

"Why not? I might already be dying."

"Crying won't help. You end up with a bad headache and swollen eyes."

"What do you know about it?"

"Obviously more than you."

"Oh, you've had such a tough life."

"Cruelty loses friends. Is that what you're aiming for?"

"NO!" Damiano shouted through the tears. "I want this over with."

Matte approached Damiano cautiously and laid both hands on her shoulders. "That I understand. A day and a half. Then you can celebrate wildly or cry as much as you want."

"Why is everything so neat and tidy for you, Pierre?"

He hugged her tightly. "It's not. It never was."

"Thanks for that."

"You're welcome. I have news to add to our investigation. Before I get to that, I called the hospital. Tibbett is still semi-comatose. The brother has been there at her side."

"I'd guess care and ulterior motives."

"I'd agree."

"It didn't take the school kids long to determine that Andrew Anderson was the driver responsible for the Emma Tibbett crash. We have already learned the boy was fourteen and he wasn't speeding."

"Just stupid with dire consequences."

"Now I've learned that Anderson and the Tibbett boys attend the same school. Last night Michael was called by a friend who revealed the identity. Tibbett found the address and launched a brick through their front window. Fortunately, no one was injured. Police were called. Around three-thirty this morning, Michael Tibbett rang their doorbell, tearfully confessed and paid for the deductible. Best to come. Mr. Anderson and his wife cancelled the charges, and he actually drove the boy home. Life!"

"Good people. Why don't we meet them?"

"Sometimes we do and don't realize it. In every case, there are good people. There are two pretty good people in this room."

"You can't count us!"

"But I do."

"I have come across the word 'frustration' too many times," Damiano said, with a note of defeat. We seem to be repeating the paths already walked. I think we should forget Maggie Barrett. We're stretching with her. We have Connor Tibbett, Sandra Hughes and Brian Barrett, all strong motives, no alibis. We start with each of them again. We try to learn something not previously investigated. Do you agree?"

"I never cut anyone off, but we'll start again with those three. One of them is a murderer."

"You think it's murder."

"Not entirely sure of anything on the case. But it's one more day for you. Try to get some sleep." For the first time in days, Matte took full measure of his partner. Damiano was a stunning woman in her forties. Her thick dark hair was swept back behind her ear with a golden clasp. Her shoulders were broad and contoured in her black cashmere sweater. Her assets, as she jokingly referred to them, were the envy of men and women alike. Today, she was wearing charcoal slacks pinstriped with black. A classy black boot enhanced her height. Though Matte was gay, he had a strong eye for feminine beauty. The only indication of her inner fear he saw mirrored in her eyes because he knew her. *Trust Toni to dress well even if the world might come crashing down on her.*

He smiled fondly as he closed the door and left her to her own thoughts.

CHAPTER TWENTY-NINE

CONNOR TIBBETT HAD managed to work quickly and early, not an easy feat considering the volatility of the market and the ten percent overall loss to most portfolios he oversaw. By ten thirty, he was back at the hospital, his visits extended to three minutes. He had a clear plan for the day. At that moment, he was whispering into Emma's ear, "You know I'd never hurt you, Emma. I'm your brother." The male nurse at the nursing station happened to glance at Emma's monitor and noticed immediately that her blood pressure was rising enough to alarm him. He rushed into the room, startling Connor.

"She's having a rough go. Mr. Tibbett, what did you say to her?"

His words struck Connor like an inquisition. "My sister and I were arguing before the accident, family stuff. Believe me I learned my lesson. I was trying to comfort her, and I didn't mean to disturb her. I am so sorry."

"Well, I think you both could use a break. I know her sons and husband will be here this afternoon."

"Ex-husband."

"Whatever." The ICU nurse, usually friendly, had taken a dislike to Connor, perhaps more like a distrust. "Right now, my patient need rest and quiet."

"Fine. I have work to attend to. I do want to be here when Emma wakes up. I have been at her side since the accident, and I'll be quiet." He purposely accentuated 'quiet'. His demeanor hardened with the tone of his words. He left thinking this just might work out. The boys are in school, so the house is empty.

The commute to Pointe Claire was faster than he had anticipated. He drove south on Highway 13 and headed west along the Trans-Canada until he cut off at Sources Boulevard. Devon's car wasn't in the driveway. The coast was clear, and he remembered that Emma hid the extra key wrapped with black electrical tape at the bottom of the brass mailbox that was not used anymore. He let himself in the front door. The neighbors knew him. There wouldn't be a problem. He locked the door behind him. The bedroom, that's the place the book had to be. First, he remembered to look in clear sight. That was usually where one found a lost item. He checked all four sides of the mattress without any luck. The drawers offered up nothing. His search led to further panic. The closets. Two! *God, look at the shoeboxes!*

He moved quickly and began pulling down three at a time. He knelt on the ground and tore off the tops, trying to keep a mental note to recall what top went with each box. The longer he looked for the agenda, the more he fretted there was damaging information in it. He hadn't even touched the second closet. He yanked the last four boxes to the floor.

Connor didn't hear the key turning in the lock, but he heard the front door open.

"Connor, you here?"

Devon made some noise before he mounted the stairs. Connor threw three of the boxes into the closet, but Devon found him on his knees with a telltale box. Devon knew exactly why his brother-in-law was there. "What are you doing here?"

"I could ask you the same question. The doctors think Emma might wake up today. I am looking for some comfortable clothes."

"In a shoebox?"

"What do I know about women's clothes?"

"I can see that."

Connor had not closed the closet. "Why are *you* here?"

"Groceries."

"Playing the dad."

"I'm trying to be. Are you looking for something, Connor?"

"Look, Devon. You're nobody in this house, just a guy playing dad who'll desert the boys when you tire of them. Isn't that what you did to my sister?"

"I'm asking about your snooping, Connor."

"I don't answer to you."

"I know you scared Emma. She was still shaking about the police and you when we had dinner."

"I didn't mean to scare her. That was stupid on my part."

"Don't worry, she didn't share what you said with me. She's loyal to you."

"All I said to her was to stop giving up any information to the police. They have a way of taking words out of context."

"I think you said more to her than that. Emma is not a hysterical woman."

Connor's face contorted. "Since when are you the protector of this family? You deserted both Emma and the kids when Terry was born. You're divorced – you have no business here in the first place."

"Why are you changing the subject?"

"I'm not changing anything, Devon. You have groceries. and I'm looking for clothes."

"I think the boys already thought of that. By the way, I think I might know what you're looking for."

"I was looking for clothes," he screeched in Devon's face.

"Right. Try to calm down." He looked Connor square in the eye. "You won't find it." Devon smiled and went downstairs to unpack the groceries.

"Wait!"

Devon didn't.

"*Wait!*"

CHAPTER THIRTY

SANDRA HUGHES HAD been more troubled by the detectives' call and questioning than she had let on. Both had disturbed an equilibrium built with tears and determination. Old memories returned swirling in her head. The anxiety that came with a loss of control hovered like a wasp. She walked across the hall to the studio apartment she had rented along with her own two-room unit. The studio had given her a new life and career. It was also a place to hide and shelter from the chaos that rocked her days and stalked her dreams years after James died. Sandra hated the word 'passed'. Dying made a statement with dignity.

Sandra walked over to the window and looked down on Seigniory Avenue already lined with cars, people visiting the hospital who had found free parking. An Amazon van had temporarily parked in front of her building. Turning, she went over to her stool. Unable to prevent herself, she rose and walked to the closet and unlocked its door. The storage unit was relatively deep. And it took Sandra some time to lift out the neatly-labelled cardboard boxes one by one. The last box, well hidden, was incorrectly labelled "canvasses and incidentals." Sitting on the round carpet, crossed legged, she split the white tape with a handy knife and lifted out all the files of James's case, the final journey of his life.

Sandra reached for the first folder, although she had memorized what it contained long ago. Opening it, she began to reread the first of many letters received from James's school commission that struck like fire bombs. "We regret to inform you, Mr. James Hughes, that you have been formally charged with forgery in regards to your yearly evaluation, September 20, 1997. Please present yourself at the office of the school commission one week from today, at ten-thirty."

She clearly recalled that James read the letter and handed it to her. "First, they think I might drink in the afterhours at school. He was carrying a glass of wine while there might have been a student still in the school. It was not a fact, but a possibility. Now this!"

"We need a lawyer."

"The woman ticked the wrong box. A simple mistake."

"Will she admit that?"

"When hell freezes over."

"Exactly…" My remark was superfluous. The rumor of the evaluation forgery spread like gossip does, blowing it out of proportion the next day.

"We definitely need a lawyer." he admitted soberly. "Are you prepared for that? I did nothing wrong, Sandra." James was preoccupied with health issues. He took longer to feel the clutch of this danger.

"This is serious, James."

"I can't believe any of this."

"We have to start."

First, the anonymous letter accusing negligent behavior, the alleged forgery and on and on. Even when the forensic specialist from the RCMP declared the evaluation was not forged, James thought the case was closed, over. It wasn't. The board deleted the charge and found a new one. Permitting teachers time off paid for by petty cash, or other means. Principals were afraid to admit they had done the very same thing because they feared for their jobs. James was isolated.

Sandra didn't bother finishing the contents of the folder. Reaching for the second brought tears as hot as they had been years ago. There were two letters from his surgeons. "Mr. James Hughes is undergoing extreme stress at this precarious time in his life. The initial melanoma has metastasized to the lungs and kidneys. His chances of seeing the year through are minimal at best. Would it not be possible to delay additional stress to allow him whatever peace he can muster at such a time?"

How ironic Sandra thought. Neither she nor James recognized the reality of his imminent death, they were stalwart in the determination to fight. Folder after folder Sandra read what she already knew, but each blow struck a new bruise. When she opened the last folder, she saw the letters, the two she had saved. The identical letters, save the top names. How fortunate she was to have a good friend like Stephanie who listened to mad thoughts and understood. What had she said, "You're innocent until you're indicted? That goes for everyone."

Sandra had watched a Woody Allen film where Woody had been given magic dust that helped him disappear for fifteen minutes. She'd use that dust and attend a school board meeting, invisibly. Once behind the admin woman, Anita Strong, she'd bonk her on the back of her head. Quickly and unseen, she'd run from the room, All Steph did was laugh and say, "That's so beneath you!"

There were darker plans she shared when everything hurt, knowing they'd be safe with Steph who understood blowing off steam. Steph knew it was only talk. She blew her fair share of steam. Who would ever envision Stephanie being struck and killed by a city bus? She never used a bus. A bus!

Steph had been that kind of best friend one enjoyed only in childhood. She had jumped off the high balcony with Sandra to boast to all her friends they had done the jump together, and she kept secrets. They both did. Loneliness fell to another level when Steph died. The single consolation was that her mad secrets were gone too. Quietly, Sandra neatly stacked the boxes and returned them to the storage unit. Turning away from the past, Sandra walked back to her apartment. She couldn't think of colors or brushes.

CHAPTER THIRTY-ONE

CONNOR RUSHED DOWN the stairs after Devon who headed to the kitchen. He took one step after him and decided against the move. There was nothing to gain but further embarrassment. He slammed the front door so hard it shook on its hinges. Devon placed the hot chicken with the gravy-soaked potatoes in the oven on low heat, and left the can of peas out on the counter. After he put the bread, frozen dinners, milk and apples away, he drove to St. Thomas High School.

Devon sat in the car waiting. He spotted Michael first, probably because he was hobbling on crutches. He got out of the car and met him. "What happened?"

"I'll tell you, but not with the kids around. Okay?"

"Whatever is best."

Bobby and Terry ran to the car and did a double take when they saw Michael. "What happened…"

"I missed the last stair. Thought I had broken my knee."

"Did ya?" Terry wanted to know.

"Drop it."

"Alright."

It took a third try to find a parking space. They walked briskly to the trauma center. Devon said, "Bobby, go first, then Terry. Talk to your mom, tell her you love her and miss her. You guys know what to say. I need to speak to Mike."

Devon and Michael walked down the hall for privacy.

"Luke called me last night with the name and address of the kid who crashed Mom."

"So, you went to the house and you did what exactly?"

Michael dropped his head. "I threw a brick through the front window."

"You know what a sucker punch is?"

"Yeah."

"What you did was worse – that was the work of a coward!"

"I wanted to show Mom that no one could hurt or kill her and get away with it, not as long as I am around."

"And the knee?"

"I tripped, running home and my knee crashed against the curb. Now I have to get an X-ray."

"Do you even know if the police came?"

Michael took his time and finished the story.

"You could have killed someone!" Devon whispered. "You are one lucky SOB!"

"I gave them five hundred bucks."

"I guess your heart was in the right place. That's what a good man does. But remember the kid that caused the accident didn't mean to hurt your mother. But you intended to inflict harm."

"Don't tell Bobby or Terry."

"I won't."

From inside the ICU, they heard an excited show from Terry. "Mom opened her eyes and she looked right at me!"

They rushed to Emma's room but couldn't enter until Terry came out. "See, nurse, Mom is waking up! She's waking up!" Terry's face lit up with joy.

Terry, flushed, ran out to tell Michael and Devon. "Bobby, would you let Michael go in before you."

"I guess, but it's not fair."

Michael held a wet facecloth to Emma's lips.

"I've called the doctor, and I'll get some ice chips," the attending nurse told him.

"Mom. You're back. We all love you." Tears streamed down his cheeks in single lines.

Two doctors arrived, examined the patient and decided they should remove the tubing that assisted her breathing. "You should leave, son."

"I won't, but I'll step to the other side. I want to hold my mother's hand."

"Mrs. Tibbett, take a deep breath now. Hold it. Now, let it out slowly. Good." The tubes were out.

Emma coughed twice and then began to breathe.

Michael kissed his mother's forehead and left. "The others want to see you, Mom."

Bobby broke down before he reached her. "I thought you were going to die. And, and, you're not! You showed them, Mom." Bobby wore his winning smile and kissed his mother.

Terry just stood at the side of the bed. "I was the first to see you wake up."

Emma did her best to smile at her youngest although her throat was sore and dry.

Devon was the last in the room. "Well, Em, it's hard to put an old horse down."

Emma did smile though she felt her lips crack. "The boys are terrific, thanks to you. They even cleaned their rooms for you. I'm sticking around to help, so you take all the time you need. You're quite a woman, I…"

Emma smiled again.

Devon was about to say that her agenda was safe with him. But he knew it was not the right time to bring up the subject.

"Connor was here for two days. I'm here. So don't let him frighten you or bully you. Do you hear me, Em?"

"Saafe." That was the best Emma could do on a dry throat.

"Yes. Can I steal a kiss?"

"Yeaa."

The boys drove to the Radimed Clinique on Frobisher in Pointe Claire, hoping Michael could be a walk-in. After all, Emma worked there. Michael was lucky. After the X-ray he was told to stay off the foot. The doctor's office would call with results.

By the time Connor reached the hospital, he was told the good news, but Emma was finally sleeping and they did not wish to wake her. "A real bummer! After all the time I put in, I wasn't there when it counted." He felt the boys and Devon were now teamed up against him. He took a chance and called Timothy.

"You have some gall calling me after telling me to get lost. There's nothing here for you."

"Believe it or not, I miss you. I strike out at the wrong people."

"You've heard of a bridge too far?"

"I have."

"You've taken it. And, when did you discharge my .22?"

"When we went to the Laurentians, ages ago, remember?"

"Bullshit! Connor, listen hard. Don't ever call me again."

CHAPTER THIRTY-TWO

WHEN THE PHONE RANG, Sandra's thoughts were still askew. She reached for her iPhone with some hesitancy. It was a mistake to go through the files. Their painful memories engulfed her for the rest of the day, burning like indigestion. "Yes?"

"Sandra, I hope you remember me, Martin Heron, Stephanie's brother. It's been twenty years, but it doesn't seem that long to me."

"We met at Steph's funeral. Of course, I remember you. Steph sometimes talked about her younger brother." *Steph referred to him as 'he of wild imagination or is it hallucination?'*

The hair on the back of Sandra's neck rose as they passed through the niceties before getting to the point.

"I'll get to the reason of my call. I need a huge favor of you."

"Would you like to meet for coffee?"

"No, that wouldn't be a good idea."

"Well, go ahead."

"I read that the police have reopened the Tibbett case. Mom is eighty-three. She's doesn't hear well anymore and is riddled with arthritis, but her mind is sharp as a tack. Steph and she were very close. My mom was nobody's fool, she knew Steph had problems, but as with the dead, only the good is recalled."

"You're losing me, Martin."

"The night the Tibbetts died, Steph and you were out together. For whatever reason, she drove back to my place shaken up and crying. She wouldn't tell me what happened. All she cried was, 'I should never have gone.' I don't care what happened that night, I am begging you not to bring Steph's name up if anything happens to you. News like that would kill my mother. It would just kill her."

"Are you accusing us of something?"

"What I said was that whatever occurred, I don't want to know. I want Steph protected."

"Well, I will disclose what we did that night to ease your blatant suspicions."

"I repeat. What you did or didn't do is none of my business – keep my sister out of it, or so help me God…"

Sandra stood and paced around the apartment. "I listened to you – now listen to me. Fair?"

"Not if it concerns that case."

"It doesn't. Before I begin, you have the days wrong. It was ten years ago. Steph and I were together on Wednesday night not Thursday. What Stephanie was upset about was going to the Holiday Inn. Steph had an on and off again relationship with a lawyer in Ottawa. He apparently said he would leave his wife. Steph had just been disappointed, not devastated, in another relationship and contacted him. He promised her again that he would leave his wife, and Steph would have a lovely gold bracelet to celebrate. She was excited for the whole week. Steph was not madly in love, but I think she finally chose to settle. That afternoon he called everything off. He said he'd realized just that day that he still loved his wife and extended family. He couldn't leave her. Steph had hurts from other relationships, as many of us do. She was fuming at his duplicity, the nerve of it. The cowardice! 'He's going to buy me that bracelet.' Though I told her not to be foolish, he wasn't worth her anger. She drove to Fairview Shopping Centre and bought herself a gold band from Galazzo Jewelry. A day later, he was in Montreal, booked at the Holiday Inn in Pointe Claire to meet a client. Steph got it in her mind she'd catch him at the hotel and force the 'bugger' to pay for the bracelet. I told her she was humiliating herself. But her mind was dead set.

"I went in with her and hung around the lobby for the fallout. Her face was crimson when she stepped out of the elevator. I went to her immediately to prevent a scene. 'He brought the bitch with him. I told him he better follow me down to the lobby, or I'd go back up to their room!' I told her we should leave, but she was furious. About ten minutes later, he emerged from the elevator, walked over to the ATM machine and withdrew the cash. He told her to open her hands and he counted each bill loudly for people to hear, 'There, Honey, that's it!' Steph looked at the money and then she threw the bills in his face. He almost fell over backwards. She ran out, and I ran after her.

"We didn't speak about what happened. There was no point. She dropped me off at the corner. I gather she drove to your place that night."

"I know that's possible because I know some of that grief. Who doesn't? You haven't convinced me that wasn't the night of the murders, or that's what happened. You and Steph were great story tellers, my mother used to say."

Sandra chose not to hear his last sentence. The idiot had the day wrong! "There were men interested in Steph, but *she* chose her men and she accepted the pitfalls, even married men and their silly lies. I admired her independence and strength."

"I just want to protect my mother. Give me your promise that my sister's name won't come up in the investigation."

"There is no need for it to come up. No need for either of us to come up. You're insulting me. I know now you don't trust me."

"It doesn't matter that I don't trust you. You're of no consequence to me. I'm sorry for my sister, but Steph is gone now, and I can't help her. It's my mother who counts. I still have that goading hunch, so I need your promise. I know something as well of what you and you husband went through. From what I did hear, I'd want to kill somebody."

"So did I at times, but Steph and I never could figure out the perfect crime. We constructed magic plots. They were nonsense, for God's sake! I wasn't about to give those bastards a chance at my life. I also didn't have it easy after James died. Infections, surgery and grief that is still with me."

"Steph said you were a person of your word. Just promise. As you know, I wasn't always kind to Steph, but I want to protect my mother and her now."

"For God's sake, Martin, I promise."

"And I thank you."

Sandra knocked her stool over when Martin hung up.

CHAPTER THIRTY-THREE

DAMIANO LINGERED IN the murder room in an attempt to delay the evening. "Pierre, we know that the distribution of Stu Tibbett's will was traditional, but we don't know if there were intended changes."

"It's a good point. Go home. I can get in touch with the lawyer."

When Damiano hadn't moved, Matte repeated, "Toni, go home, try to get some rest."

"Like that's possible. I'm sorry. I know I'm being a pout."

"You've been braver than I thought you'd be. Good luck. Call me if you can."

"I will, either way." With that she was off. As soon as she reached home, she showered and sat on the corner of her bed. "There is nothing wrong with me! There can't be. There just can't be." She stood up and stretched and repeatedly drew in deep breaths.

Jeff had quietly appeared in the doorway. "Toni, if you continue doing that, you can pass out. How about a spinach omelet with asparagus and sourdough toast?"

"For dinner?"

"For your nerves."

"Sounds good. Jeff, I don't feel much like talking."

"Didn't figure you would."

"It's not you or Luke."

"We get it."

The dinner was oddly quiet, except for small talk between Jeff and Luke. Ironically, time passed as quickly as it always does. In the bedroom, Damiano lay on her back, eyes wide open. Jeff reached over to comfort her, but she jumped nervously. "Please don't, I feel smothered."

"Do you want the bed to yourself?"

"NO! I want you here."

"Okay."

Damiano tried sleeping on her stomach when her back didn't work. Neither side worked. The sheet and blanket were balled into a giant mess that she didn't bother to fix. "Are you asleep?"

"Nope, waiting with you."

"Thanks. We're in this together." Jeff was grateful when light speared through any opening it could find. They heard the shower and knew Luke was already up. Their strapping son had many qualities, but being quiet was not one of them.

"Can we take your Merc, Dad? There's more leg room."

Jeff followed Toni. "Does anyone want coffee or toast?"

"*No!*"

"Toni, are you sure you don't want me with you?"

"I'm not sure of anything, but I want to be on my own. I need to deal with the results alone. Can you understand?"

"Your way?"

"Yes. It's all I can bear. Let's go, Luke."

"At least, give me a kiss."

"There." A butterfly kiss, close to a miss entirely.

Jeff watched them back out of the driveway and then he walked back into the house.

To Luke's credit, he looked over at his mother and did not say a single word until they reached Pine Avenue. With a sharp U-turn, that shook Damiano, Luke backed the Jeep perfectly, in one motion, into a parking space. "Do you want me to wait here for you, Mom? Mom?"

Damiano had been lost to the scenery she'd never took the time to appreciate. *So much missed!* "Do you mind, Luke?"

"Yes, but I think I understand." *I love you.*

Damiano remembered to follow the instructions, as did all the nervous patients awaiting results. Walk straight down the hall, and you see an open office. Walk around behind it, hand in your hospital card and ten dollars. Damiano waited for what she thought would be a sealed envelope that she intended to open alone in the bedroom. A small moan left her throat when she saw the printer spit out a single sheet with what, fifteen lines? No envelope – no protection against the truth.

Quickly, she folded the sheet after noticing a red star, something to herald the impending disaster. *It's so cold! Brutal.* Damiano hurried by the ill, orderlies, nurses and people like her until she was running back to the car. Luke jumped out and held the door open.

"You didn't look, Mom."

"I can't till I get home. Besides there are things I want to see along the way." Holding the sheet in her hand while Luke drove, she tried to read the report that was upside down. Nothing dangerous that she could make out. "Stop at the next corner, Luke, I want to get out of the car."

"You sure?"

"I am."

"Okay then." Luke pulled over as soon as he could.

Damiano got out of the car, turned her back to him, and read the report: "No hypermetabolic abnormality in head or neck. Spleen, pancreas and adrenals grossly unremarkable. Re the RUL lung nodule, no significant metabolic activity. This can be followed by a CT scan." Her shoulders dropped, and Luke ran around the car to give her a bear hug. "What does it say?"

"I'm okay. I'M OKAY!" In seconds mother and son were laughing and crying.

"We have to tell Dad."

"And Pierre."

"Okay, get back in the car. It's so fantastic!"

"It's a second chance." She called Jeff. "I'm good!"

"Thank God! Get home."

"We're on our way." When his phone rang, Matte picked up immediately.

"That's the best news I've had all year."

"I'll owe you big time."

"No, you won't. 'That's what friends are for, keep smiling, keep shining…'"

"I didn't know you could sing."

"My dear, I have many talents you don't know about. By the way, you were right on. I have news about the will."

"I'll be there by noon. Right now, I want to be home."

Jeff was waiting outside the house. It was a long hug. "I have breakfast waiting."

"Lots of everything?"

"And cuddling tonight."

"Sleep is all I want tonight, and you."

"I'll give Luke a hand with the dishes and come right up." Five minutes later, Jeff bounded up the stairs to find Toni across the bed, sleeping deeper than a rock. He left the bedroom and called Matte. "Hi! Yes, so lucky. Thanks for your help, Pierre. Luke tells me Toni said she'd be in at noon. I couldn't wake her if I tried. Make that tomorrow morning. She hasn't slept in many nights."

"My Ativan didn't help?"

"Your Ativan?"

"I gave her one a night."

"So did I. What a rascal I married! And that's putting it mildly."

"Part of her charm." Matte laughed.

"I am so relieved to have my girl back, and we are not preparing to do battle with cancer. I will be grateful for health every day. I've taken so much for granted. You are a remarkable friend, Pierre."

"It goes both ways."

CHAPTER THIRTY-FOUR

MARTIN HERON KNEW immediately he had just made a potentially costly mistake. How he wished he could cancel that call. If by any chance this Hughes and his sister were involved with the murdered couple, then he had just alerted Hughes that he was a danger to her. Once Steph died, Hughes must have believed she was in the clear. Thanks to him, she knew she wasn't. He had made certain they didn't meet one another, but it would take Hughes no time at all to locate him and his address. Steph must have mentioned he practiced law.

He couldn't go to the police because he meant what he said about protecting his mother. A new plan had to be devised to protect himself. First, he thought, he would try to dispel the growing fear that he was manufacturing. Steph's furniture had been given away years ago, but his mother had saved six cardboard boxes that he had stored in the basement of her triplex in Montreal West. He'd begin there. If he came across a gold bracelet, it might not be the one just as easily as it could be the one. Steph didn't like to throw anything out, leaving Martin a chance of finding notes and names.

He arrived at his mother's home, a hundred-year-old brown brick with an interior staircase that led to the second rented unit. His mother had the bottom floor apartment. She was in the kitchen working on her Wonderword in the *Gazette*. "I didn't hear you come in."

"I didn't want to alarm you. How are you?"

"Not as good as I'd like, but better than most."

"Good! Do you remember that Mont Blanc pen I lost around the time of Steph's death?"

"Not really, Son, there was too much grief to recall small incidentals."

"I liked that pen, and I never found it. I was wondering if I dropped it in one of the boxes of Steph's things. The pen was in my top pocket. Would it bother you if I checked them to see if I can find the pen? I'll put everything back in order."

"Seems to me like a violation of sorts. Those boxes are all I have left of Stephanie."

"I packed them with you, and we took great care. I'll do the same this time."

"Well, see that you do. Will you stay for lunch? I'll make my grilled cheese sandwiches and heat up some tomato soup. That's what I made for you both for lunch when you were children."

"I know, for old memories."

"At times, you surprise me, Son."

Martin knew he had to work quickly because his mother was keeping track and might call a halt to his search at any time. He found an old box of notes, all neatly bound with elastic. He read through most of them quickly, a litany of hopes dashed, mostly curt and final. Others, kind. Some names he even recalled. He put that box aside and looked for jewelry. Steph didn't have a lot; she didn't care much for jewelry. He remembered he had packed what she had in a shoebox. Four rings, all silver, except for her wedding ring; a simple gold band from a marriage that didn't last four years; two inexpensive chains; and two watches, somewhat better. He saw one bracelet, silver. He found what he wanted, a Galazzo blue velvet box containing a gold bracelet – this one with its turbulent story. Martin didn't know which wrenched his heart more, his sister's closed casket, or the meager possessions we all leave behind.

Overcome with loneliness and hollowness, Martin hid the notes in the inside pocket of his jacket, and put the box in his back pocket. Galazzo might keep records, but he was too overwhelmed to start his search immediately. A grilled cheese looked good to him, comfort food and a delaying tactic. He replaced the boxes in order and came upstairs. "No luck!"

His mother paused before taking a bite of the hot grilled cheese. "I don't understand why my Stephanie had such a difficult time finding a good man. Both of my children were intelligent, and your father and I had a good marriage."

Martin bit his tongue. It was unfair to do battle with the old. It's another form of bullying.

"Stephanie was brilliant and funny, even charming. Next to her, you were a dullard."

Martin had drawn blood and hated the taste. "I know you're kidding."

"Huh! Where is your wife?"

"Really, Mom? That's a long time ago. She's in Toronto. People get divorced, often."

"Huh!"

"I have to go."

"But you haven't finished, Martin?"

"I have." Martin tried to remember a time when he'd left his mother feeling good. What did she used to say, 'You're a nosey little boy?' He wanted to shout in his mother's face. *There are reasons, Mom, for our problems!* He had work to do at his office in Old Montreal, but it would have to wait. He drove to his condo, Perspectives Bates, a chic building bordering both the Town of Mount Royal and Outremont. His condo was street level, surrounded by trees and a perfect place for his electric bike and his carbon fiber Specialized when he wanted more exercise. It afforded him a clear view of the University of Montreal. He was happy here and secure. He sat at his hand-crafted designer table and spread the notes he took from his mother's house across it. Sadly, he saw they were mostly from Steph, notes she never sent. He found six others from a Kenneth Moore, sent over the years, sent from Ottawa. He reached for the velvet box and pulled the bracelet from it. The bracelet was secured in a velvet carboard backing to protect it from being scratched. Under it, he saw the folded sheet. Steph had written down the date of his call and the printed word 'BASTARD'.

What would Martin learn from the bastard? Regret, maybe, but too late. The date of the note told him it was two days before the shootings. Would Steph have been so angry that she would have driven Hughes to the home? Maybe, if she didn't know what was about to happen?

"Oh God!" One of Steph's men owned a gun, and she had boasted to him that Bob had taken her to a shooting range. She outshot Bob and all the shooters that day! There was no way Steph would have murdered two people for her friend – no way! And yet, a ten-year friendship broke up soon after. Four months later, Steph was killed in a horrible accident. "Oh my God!"

Martin sat trembling. He jumped up suddenly and locked both doors. There were cameras on all the units, but that meant little to guys with hoodies. He knew that he was frightening himself with his own scenario. But he was determined to watch his back every minute. It was all rubbish! Why not take Hughes's word. Would either of them risk their own lives? And yet, had they? The killings remained unsolved, and Steph was dead.

He couldn't risk calling the police. He had to do what? That was it. WHAT?

When another terrifying thought struck him like a punch, he rushed to his laptop. The search for the 2000 bus accident that took the life of a young woman took seconds for the story to appear. The accident occurred at the intersection of Sherbrooke Street and Decarie Boulevard. The victim stepped out onto the road as soon as the green walk light signaled. The bus driver began his right turn before he had the green go-ahead and struck the victim, dragging her about thirty feet before he heard the horrified screams of the two pedestrians who'd run after the bus. No foul play was determined. The driver and witnesses were taken to the hospital and treated for shock. No charges were filed. Martin slumped on his chair. "There should have been charges! At least, Steph wasn't pushed."

Martin knew he was frightening himself, but he couldn't stop. He never could.

CHAPTER THIRTY-FIVE

CONNOR WAS IN A SLOW BURN. Dismissed from Emma's side because hospital staff discerned that he was upsetting her and then being caught like a thief at her home rummaging through shoeboxes in her bedroom. He laughed harshly. *I suppose that's what's called not exactly running the table.* In spite of his blunders, he also possessed a hidden charm that he'd use when he felt rejected, and it generally worked.

When he was sure Devon and the family were back home, he drove to the hospital. He waited almost two hours to speak to an attending doctor. "I am the only adult family my sister has. I care deeply for my sister, and I want to know what lies ahead for her so that I can make the necessary preparations. She is a single working mother of three boys, teenagers."

"I understand, Mr. Tibbett. We have scheduled surgery for early morning to repair the tibia fracture." He checked his file. "Fortunately, the fracture was clean. We will insert a metal rod to support and set the bone. A long cast will have to be worn for six weeks, replaced later by a Sarmiento cast for a four-month period in order to ensure a full recovery. Your sister has a long road ahead of her."

"Are you suggesting rehab? To be honest, I fear a depression might well set in if my sister spends months in rehab. Those boys are her life, and this period has been an added stress for both of us." Briefly, he relayed the information about the reopening of the family murder/suicide.

"That's a difficult situation indeed. My work will be done after the surgery and final checkup. I believe Mrs. Beauchamp, head nurse of after-care, is working today." He made a quick call. Connor noticed the fatigue in the doctor's eyes and the grayish cast to his face that hadn't seem much rest or fresh air. "Thank you, Denise. He'll be in the waiting room of the ICU." The doctor turned, "I have other work I must attend to. Good luck to you."

"Thanks, Doctor." The head nurse arrived about thirty minutes later, and she was weary as well. Everyone had read about the burnout in the health care system courtesy of the pandemic, causing staff and budget shortages. It was quite different to see the wear and tear up close. Connor almost felt guilty asking her for help. Almost.

"Well, I'll get in touch with the CLSC clinic in Pointe Claire and have someone visit the home three times a week. For the two additional days there is a cost to you, but it's minimal. They will help bathe, clothe, and do some laundry. There are volunteer sitters you can have twice a week. A nurse will also make home calls for blood work if necessary. There are drivers…"

"I'll see to that. Her ex is stepping up and taking care of groceries. Her sons are good kids."

"Sounds like your sister will be in good hands."

"With your help, yes, I agree. Since she will be released in three or four days, I'll get to work and buy crutches and rent a hospital bed. I hope they deliver."

"The CLSC may provide one. Find out first. Here is my card and personal number to be used for emergencies." Connor offered his in return.

He enjoyed dinner alone, feeling a modicum of stress lifting. He bought staples for the boys and drove to their home. "Hey! What happened to you, Michael?"

"I missed the last basement step, may have torn my meniscus."

"You'll need an X-ray."

"Done! Dad took me."

Connor flinched. "Well, good. I have news." Trying to regain the position he felt he'd lost with his nephews, he announced, "I made the calls, and the Medi-quip store will be delivering a hospital bed. Mike, when it arrives, help me set it up. We need sheets, pillows and blankets." They all began the work. Michael was already adept at hopping up the stairs on crutches. Terry stayed with him. Connor jumped at the opportunity.

"Terry, you remember Mom's silly agenda."

"Yeah."

"I thought she might want it with her in the hospital. It can get pretty dull, lying in a bed."

"I haven't seen it."

"Here's a secret between you and me. Fifty bucks if you find it, but don't tell Michael and Bobby, they'll want in on the reward. If we're lucky, I'll drop the agenda off at the hospital tonight."

Dogs have good noses, and so do kids. "I think Mom threw it out, because I haven't seen it." Terry couldn't hide the half smile.

A knowing look passed between uncle and nephew. "Fine. It doesn't matter. It was only a thought." s

CHAPTER THIRTY-SIX

BY THE TIME CONNOR opened his front door, he was cold and experiencing a gnawing fear that was the fate of outsiders. Emma was afraid of him. Devon had just walked back into Emma's life and won the loyalty of kids who had long given up on a father who had deserted them. Connor was alone and an arrest was now a real possibility. He had never really needed anyone, but that was his choice, he had managed quite well on his own in the past.

He made the call without much thought. Fear and a loneliness that was new to him drove the call. It went through, and he began immediately. "I know you told me never to call you, but can you give me a few minutes." When the line wasn't cut, he began. "You were the most solid, good man I ever met. I gave you little of me and took you for granted. I was never in a good relationship and I didn't know what to do when I had one. When someone actually loves me, I lose respect for him because I'm not worthy of love. I've always been that way. Are you there?"

"Go on."

"I miss you. I hate the empty house. I opened up to Em and, now after the crash, she's afraid of me."

"What crash?"

Connor related the details to Timothy. "Her ex has walked back into their lives, and I was booted from the family. I need you, Tim. People rarely change, but I will try. I'm having the recurring dreams, the usual ones of being lost and afraid and I can't get back home. In my own way, I love you. I never changed my will because you are a deserving beneficiary. You are the only person who put up with me."

"I've changed too. I'm actually okay on my own."

"I'm scared, Tim. Come back. I'll cover all your expenses. Just come back."

"Connor, I'm settled in Delray. You broke my heart."

"I know."

"No, dammit. I don't think you have the faintest idea of what that means."

"I need you. I need another chance."

"You had years!"

"God, Tim, I'm begging you."

"I know you are trying to be honest, and I respect that, but you are also afraid."

"I am. I'm afraid I will be arrested." He whispered these words.

"I assumed that from what you've told me. It's my turn to be honest. You used my gun. I know you did."

"Dammit, I admitted I did. You don't remember? When we were at Gray Rocks, I took the gun out early in the morning. You're responsible for taking it up there! I was tempted and I took it. I walked into the woods and shot and missed two squirrels. When I got back to the room, you asked, 'What was that noise?' I said it was a car backfiring because you had told me not to touch the gun. You don't remember that?"

"Not really, but that was very near the time of your parents' death."

"I had nothing to do with that. Jesus, nothing! I was stupid to touch the gun, but it was a lark. Maybe you don't remember because you were half asleep." Connor was scrambling, desperate. "Tim, I love you. You have to believe me. You never have to worry about me. I bark but I don't bite. Give me a break."

"There's work to clear up here."

"Take all the time you need, but come." Connor exhaled.

"Can I trust you, Connor?"

"Yes." Connor closed his eyes.

"I'll come back because I believe you. Don't make a fool of me again."

When Connor's phone rang a few minutes later, he thought Tim had changed his mind. "Devon?"

"I have a favor to ask of you."

"Maybe we can do something for one another."

"I owe six grand, and I only have two. I had the cash in hand, but I gave it to Em."

"You mean you owed her the back child support – you didn't give her anything."

"Blunt, but true. I have tried to help out since that accident. And, truthfully, I had no time to make up the debt."

"You mean to play the tables for it."

"Were you born a prick?"

"Think I was. So, you want me to lend or give you the four grand?"

"Yes, and I'd make good in time."

"You have the infernal agenda, right?"

"I haven't opened it."

"At heart, you're a boy scout."

"I can make you this promise. No one will see the book until I return it to Em. I know you confided in her, but I don't know if she remembered what you said."

"Here's my counter proposal. Sell your Mustang. You'll get a great return in the market. Cars are hard to come by these days."

Devon hung up. *I'll give Donnie the two grand, take the loss and hit the tables.* Calmly, he drove to Broadview to pick up the boys.

CHAPTER THIRTY-SEVEN

WHILE DAMIANO ENJOYED the repose of the lucky, Matte called Stephane Bouchard, a lawyer, at his office in Pierrefonds. Following the formal introductions, Matte asked, "You do in fact remember the Tibbetts?"

"I read newspapers, and I saw that their case was being reopened. I pulled their files in case I received a call like this."

"What can you tell me about the Tibbetts?"

"They were a nice enough couple who requested very conventional wills. I make notes about all my clients because changing wills is the norm if one lives long enough. Circumstances change."

"Did they consult you about a change? And when did they call you, do you recall?"

"Sadly, I spoke with them by phone a few days before their tragedy."

Detective Matte, always alert, dug deeper. "I'd like to hear your observations."

"Both of them had decided to leave all their money to their daughter Emma. I quote from my notes, 'My son will do very well and won't need our help, but our daughter probably will.' They never disclosed why the daughter might need more help, or if they were angry with their son. It was none of my affair. I advised them to think twice about making such a change. These decisions create bad blood between the recipients. That animosity can carry on for years and destroy what's left of the family. I've seen it all in the past twenty-one years, and I have the records to back up my claims."

"Were they able to amend their will?"

"They only had a few nights before they lost their lives."

"So, no changes to the wills were ever made?" Matte asked.

"That's very true, Detective. It doesn't mean they didn't tell their son of their plans. I recall reading just recently that the case was being reopened. I have a good memory, just made me wonder. I don't waste time on assumptions."

"But you don't know if Mr. Tibbett ever took your advice."

"I do know he was adamant, but he never called to make the change. I had also informed him that we don't do codicils anymore, we write a whole new will and that can take one month, or longer."

"Did he try to insist the changes be made without delay as though time were a factor?"

"He didn't seem to mind the delay. He was to present the changes on paper himself, so there'd be no misunderstanding."

"As you've said, you never heard from him again."

"No, not until I read what tragedy had occurred. It must be difficult for all concerned to see over ten years there is still no closure. For the police too. It's something in our nature that demands closure, although even that has its limitations. I used to think of the son and daughter, but then I'm human, and time passes, and we go on with our lives."

Matte had heard enough. "Thank you for your time."

"You're welcome."

CHAPTER THIRTY-EIGHT

MARTIN HERON KNEW he was very high strung and hated himself because he couldn't just let go of things. The immediate solution he felt was shopping along St. Catherine Street with Ogilvy's department store his destination. He needed a new sweater, and the store with its reputation for high-quality goods, would have a wide selection. Most of his stress had hidden itself when he saw that people had returned to the city. It also reminded him of the deserted city streets just a few months ago. The pandemic of 2020 had a lifespan of two and a half years. People took their time returning to downtown. The memories and fear had lingered. Their presence that day added a lightness and freedom to Martin himself. He enjoyed the hustle and the jockeying that went on in the bus while he often looked behind himself and did his best to keep a two-foot margin between himself and others.

He felt a sudden shove and was startled when he heard, "What's up with you?"

"Me?"

"Yes, stupid, you! You bumped into me."

"I'm sorry. No harm meant."

Martin had apprently jostled the passenger. They were both in their early forties, but Martin wasn't a fighter. He was the kid that was bullied because he wore glasses in grade one. He had to remind himself that he was past all that. Anyway, Martin wasn't built to fight. He was fifteen pounds overweight, wide across the seat and thick in the thighs. Slim in the shoulders and arms. In the last few years, breasts he loathed had appeared and he did his level best to hide them. He was an avid reader. And like his sister Steph, a quick study. He was a frugal man in all but sweaters.

He hadn't thought often of Steph over the last few years, but he did that day when the bus stopped and he he felt the weight of the bus against his chest. Had Steph felt the same force and fear when the bus struck her?

Before he entered the store, he made a familiar stop at the corner window to the right of the main entrance. In his childhood, clutching Steph's hand, they'd both have their noses against the window pane to have a closer look at the wonderous Christmas show. Santa rocking back and forth, smiling at the kids, Mrs. Claus knitting, and both surrounded by travelling trains and big dolls looking on. Lights and color and movement! When he was a kid, he learned that the windows had to be washed several times a day to remove the little finger and nose prints.

He hurried into the bright store, escaping those thoughts. He began looking at the imported jackets, slacks, and ties, all too pricey for him. Before he got to the sweaters, he treated himself to a tour of the newly renovated fifth floor. Gone were all the fine Egyptian sheets, the costly duvets, and custom pillows imported from Paris. A man could dream. Taking the down escalator from the fifth floor, Martin rarely thought of his inner ear problem that could cause dizziness. That day his head was clear. He was fine. Yet, more than halfway down, he felt pressure on his back and heard his own scream as he fell forward. Customers on the escalator scrambled not to fall with him. A man behind Martin grabbed his arm and pulled it back seconds before his hand would have been caught in the comb plate at the bottom of the escalator.

"Help me get him up. He could have lost his hand."

"What happened?"

Someone said, "The man went to step down and missed the stair. He'd have been safe if he hadn't moved."

"Was he sick or something?"

"I don't know. Maybe he fainted, but I'm no doctor."

Martin lay on the floor, trembling. *I felt a push!*

"I've called an ambulance," the store manager said. He'd been close to the accident and acted quickly.

"Sir, are you alright?" an employee asked. "You're damn lucky this man pulled you out of the way."

"Here's a chair. Take it easy. Were you feeling faint?" another employee asked.

"I think I just missed a step. I suppose I wasn't paying attention. I'm fine now." Martin wanted to leave. *I was pushed!*

"I think you should wait for the ambulance. A paramedic will check you out."

"I'd really like to go. I'm fine."

"Please wait to protect all concerned."

"I won't be filing any lawsuit; but I just want to leave. You can't keep me here."

"You're correct, sir."

Martin tried to appear steady on his feet. "Thank you very much for the help. I'm just a stubborn guy who wants to leave."

"As you wish. You might want to thank this gentleman for saving your hand."

Martin shook hands with the man. *Did he push me?* Outside the store, he realized his mistake. "I should have gotten his name. Then I could have found out about him." He waved a taxi down. He was too upset for another bus ride. When he reached home, he stripped. In the mirror he could see slight bruises on his back and a tiny one on his side.

"Maybe there is something here, and I'm not overreacting. I'll call the police and mention my connection to the, what's their name, how can I forget? I have to settle down. Tibbett! That's the name. I can't sound like some crazy. I might have something concrete. I am not this agitated for nothing."

CHAPTER THIRTY-NINE

ON DAMIANO'S FIRST normal day back at work, she wasn't surprised to find Matte deep into his notes. But he looked like a man who had stepped into quicksand. "Pierre, didn't you tell me yesterday that we had something? I'm guessing now that it wasn't a colossal break."

"We've never worked a case quite like this, Toni. The lawyer said that Stu Tibbett wanted to change both wills. So far, it looks like a lead. If we had discovered that Connor Tibbett knew that his father was prepared to disinherit him, then we'd have a motive. When Stu Tibbett died, in whatever manner, a few days later before any changes were made, that motive evaporated. Connor Tibbett can deny his father ever told him. Connor Tibbett looks like our man, but we can't nail him. Emma Tibbett is still in no condition to discuss such matters. The doctors wouldn't let us near her."

"We haven't stagnated in a case in a long time. Do you recall what we used to do to reboot?" Damiano would not spoil her good luck.

"Treat ourselves to a good dinner, but…"

She strode the few steps over to him. "The dinner is dedicated to a reboot and my medical results. I've already asked Jeff and Luke. They chose Gibby's and I chose Steak Frites. Jeff is treating you for your much needed help and *moi* because I will continue to annoy him as usual. What do you say, partner? You have the deciding vote."

Matte knew what Damiano wanted. "I choose Steak frites."

"There's a reason you are my partner. We'll meet you there at seven-thirty. Give us all time to digest. There was a time when I never thought of such things. Now, when I eat late, the food sits in my stomach."

"Those were the days."

"You said it my brother."

Their anticipation of the evening ahead came quickly to an end when Damiano received a call from the front desk saying that a nervous and insistent man was at the entrance asking to talk to the detectives on the Tibbetts' case.

"Well, we're batting zero. What can we lose? I'll go down and meet him." When Matte opened the door, he found an anxious man who kept looking over his shoulder to see if he was being followed.

"I'm not some crazy, but a few days ago I was just a normal guy." Matte called Damiano. "Join us in the boardroom."

"Please follow me. I'm Detective Matte of Major Crimes."

"This is a very bare room. Is it used for intimidation?"

"We use this room for interviews. The interrogation rooms on the sixth floor are far more intimidating."

Martin stood, clearly forgetting his stress and enjoying what he saw when Damiano walked into the room. Here, he'd have the full attention of major detectives. "I'm Martin Heron. I have come for two reasons: my sister's ten-year friendship with Sandra Hughes, and a sudden fear for my life."

"Perhaps you can explain the first part to us," Damiano used her disarming smile.

"It started when I read in the *Gazette* that the Tibbett case was being reopened. I always found it strange that the case wasn't quickly solved. It seemed like a pedestrian case – an average couple in suburbia."

The implied criticism was noted by Matte and Damiano.

"I am not judging. The fact that it wasn't solved suggested a perfect crime, and, somehow, I don't believe it was. My sister was struck and killed by a bus two years after the murders. Sandra and Steph were best of friends – they had stories to share. Steph was brilliant, but when it came to men, she did the choosing and suffered some of her choices. In some ways, she was ahead of her time. Sandra was dealing with her terminally ill husband who had been fired. His case was being fought in court. I didn't know the personal details. I do know people are people and colleagues were fearful of any involvement – fearful for their own jobs and families. I'm sure you've spoken to Sandra Hughes. Steph and Sandra were angry with all the bosses involved but they were not the type to actually murder anyone.

"Yet recently, I discovered something around the night of the murders, could be the actual night, I don't know. Sandra told me one of Steph's sad episodes and that's where they were that night. Again, I have no proof it was that actual night. It's probably the truth, but if it isn't, Sandra is lucky Steph is dead. If my sister was stupid enough to drive Sandra to the Tibbetts, I'm sure that she had no clue what Sandra was planning. She's safe now that Steph is gone.

"Sandra told me they had driven to the Holiday Inn that night where Steph met a man who told my sister he'd leave his wife that week. At the last minute, the mensch decided to stay with his wife, leaving Steph in the lurch. It was Steph's payback sort of thing. Apparently, she made a fool of him. The story didn't surprise me. I could have kicked myself for calling Sandra. I realized, if Sandra was the perpetrator, she could involve me in some accident, and no one would suspect foul play."

"Mr. Heron. When I met you at the entrance you were extremely nervous, and kept looking over your shoulder. Has anything actually happened to give you cause to be frightened?" Matte's tone was serious.

"I reread the events surrounding my sister's death. The bus driver turned before he had a green light, struck Steph and dragged her thirty feet before he stopped. At least Steph wasn't pushed. I was at Ogilvy's today on an escalator. There were, I believe, around nine of us close together. I have inner ear problems that sometimes cause dizzy spells. They occur if I get out of bed too quickly. I wasn't in bed today. I was on an escalator when I felt myself falling. I thought I felt a slight push. I fell five stairs. A man grabbed my hand before it was sucked into the grinders at the bottom of the escalator. I was lucky. I checked myself out fully as soon as I got home. I have bruises on my back and side. The people around me that day said I probably fainted or missed a step. So, I don't know if I'm the cause of my own fear, or if there is reason to be afraid. I can say that the fact the murders remain unsolved piqued my curiosity. I should have left matters alone."

For a few seconds, they appeared to be stumped. Damiano, she who was going to live, jumped up. "Would you mind if Detective Matte took some photos of the bruises. We can send them to forensics."

"The bruises are hardly visible. I don't mean to be a bother."

"You aren't, sir. Give me your number. I'll punch it into my phone. Good. In the meantime, vigilance is never a mistake. Stay safe."

"I'll see you out," Matte said, rising. When he got back to the boardroom, Damiano was examining the photos of the bruises. "Do you think he pushes our case forward?"

"I'm beginning to regret…"

"I'll call Ogilvy's."

Matte didn't stop her.

When Damiano explained the incident, she was transferred to the floor manager. Damiano listened for a minute "Do you think there is any possibility the man was pushed?"

"Are you inferring a lawsuit?"

"I'm Major Crimes as I explained. I need your full cooperation."

"Yes, yes. I understand. The gentlemen closest to the victim was the person who literally saved his hand, perhaps his life. It takes time to stop the escalator. Everyone who was on the escalator stayed around and tried to help. It was the victim who wanted to leave as soon as possible and refused a paramedic. They all thought he lost his footing. Two women suggested he panicked. It was an unsettling experience and an accident. The man was fortunate he suffered no serious injuries."

"You did not believe the man was pushed."

"Heavens, no. Every person on that escalator tried to help."

"Thank you for your time."

Damiano who had used speaker phone turned to Matte. "Well?"

"The manager believes it was an accident. Let's enjoy our dinner tonight and get to the work of sorting tomorrow."

CHAPTER FORTY

TIMOTHY, HIS PARTNER, would not arrive for a couple of days, and that meant that Connor could get to work. He withdrew four thousand dollars from the checking account, and pocketed the cash. He wore dark clothes with a hoodie that he hated, but would serve its purpose. He expected a long wait and could not risk exposure. Devon's apartment on Lincoln Avenue was in an older, blackened white brick building, but still presentable. Truth was, Connor knew Devon was rarely there except to sleep. Connor was well-positioned because Devon could be spotted from a good distance. The apartment building was the only one on the block, the rest of the block housed private dwellings. Connor was no amateur. As a teenager, he and a friend had broken into seven or eight garages just for the challenge, and learned to hide themselves from the cameras.

Connor took the chance that Devon hadn't sold his Mustang. He loved his car. It was probably the only tangible belonging he hadn't lost to his gambling addiction. Connor bent over and keeping his head down, took cover behind a Buick as it drove into the garage. He hid behind a white scarred pillar that had met many a bumper and lost. At least, by three-forty-one, he was out of the rain. Only people with hope called it drizzle. Four o'clock came and went, and he shuffled his feet and rubbed his hands to keep warm, and to keep his spirits from flagging. Just before five, a red Mustang entered the garage slowly, too slowly. "Good, he's got a head full," Connor thought, as he stealthily moved behind the parked cars. The Mustang turned and grazed a pillar, breaking the aluminum disk around the front light on the driver's side leaving a white scar on the red paint.

Devon pushed the car door open and fell on the grimy floor cursing and moaning. "My ribs are busted!" When Connor cautiously approached him, Devon turned his head not without difficulty. "What the fuck are you doing here?"

"I took out the four thousand you need. The door was open, so I walked in to get out of the rain."

"They got me drunk, Connor, then broke my ribs. Two grand didn't work shit."

"Let me get you to your apartment."

"Breaking and entering seems to be second nature to you."

"I'll go then – here's the cash."

"Dammit, I need your help. They used a crowbar on me."

To help him up, Connor grabbed Devon under an arm.

"Shit! The other side."

"Okay, sorry." When they finally reached #402, Devon tripped over his own legs and struck the side of his head on the corner of the coffee table. A trickle of blood appeared on his temple. Connor half dragged half lifted him to the sofa and hoisted his legs up as well. Should he call an ambulance? He stared down at Devon – he was breathing painfully. He wanted the agenda. Help could wait. While Devon moaned on the sofa, Connor began to search the apartment. Where the hell would a gambler hide anything? A sly smile crossed his lips. The freezer under meat! He rushed to the fridge, opened the stocked freezer, and turned over two frozen chickens at the back. *Le voila!* The agenda was locked, and he had no key. He used a knife to break the lock and began reading.

"That's what you wanted all along," Devon shouted hoarsely from the sofa.

"My sister wants me arrested! She exaggerated every word. It's a lie, all of it as she's written it. She was so scared the police would nail her for obstruction that she told them everything and sacrificed me in the process."

"She was frightened, but you can't go ahead and destroy the agenda or take it."

"Why not? You're going to stop me?"

"I promised the boys I'd protect their mother's privacy."

"Forget their trust, you can rebuild it. I can't go to prison. Do you hear me?"

Without warning, Devon's skin turned gray as he coughed up light bubbles of blood.

"Jesus!"

He gasped for breath, turning his head from side to side, blood flying out of his mouth.

Connor stood watching as he had done with his father. *This is just like Dad!*

"Get help!" Devon tried to say.

Connor had seen the same awful desperation in his father's eyes. "You'll die, Devon, if I don't get you to a hospital. A rib must have punctured a lung. Soon, you won't be able to breathe."

"Please…"

"I'll call an ambulance." Connor tore out that last page of the agenda.

Devon continued coughing, but the coughs were becoming weaker. Connor reached for his phone and stabbed in the number. "What? He'll be dead in an hour! I'll drive him." He hung up, grabbed the money and stuffed it in his pocket. He ran to the fridge and placed the agenda where he had found it, minus the one page. "Listen, you have to help me and stay awake." He took hold of Devon and almost fell with the dead weight. "Help me, Devon! Don't you dare fall asleep." They made it to the garage, and Connor dragged Devon to the car and pushed him onto the front seat.

The coughing had almost stopped. "Devon, stay with me! You'll make it." He ran three red lights before he was pulled over. When the officer saw the plight of the injured man, he turned on his sirens and led the rush to the Glen Hospital, minutes away. When Connor pulled into emergency, the officer followed. Devon was lifted to the gurney and rushed into the hospital down the hall.

Connor and the officer waited together. "What happened?" the officer asked while taking out his pad.

"He owed money and only had part of it. The sharks he owed beat him badly, used a crowbar. I went to lend him the balance owing, but he wasn't home. As I was leaving, I spotted his car. It's hard to miss a red Mustang. When his car came to a stop in the garage, the door of the car opened, and he fell onto the garage floor, and I mostly carried him to his place. You know the rest. It was an hour wait for an ambulance, so I drove him here."

"I don't think he was breathing," the officer said. "You should call family if he has one."

"He was breathing, but shallow, like wheezing." Connor could hear pounding blood in his temples. He couldn't call the kids at that time. He stood and tried to digest the events of the night.

"Do you know the names of the sharks he owed the money to?"

"God, no. He's my ex-brother-in-law and I haven't seen him in three years. I never saw the logic in gambling. He worked at the casino here, like that was a help to his addiction!" He was about to add something when he saw the doctor in scrubs heading his way.

"We did what we could. The patient was not breathing when he arrived. Sorry for your loss. The office person will need information from you, then she will direct you to the nurse who will give you his personal belongings."

"I'm not his family. She can keep them."

"Do you know the family?"

"My sister, but she's been in a car accident." What little reserve Connor had was lost. "Wait a minute!' Connor shouted, as if shouting could roll back the tragedy. "He just died, just like that? I was talking to him minutes ago. What the hell!"

"I'm sorry, sir."

Connor couldn't comprehend his tears and swiped at them with the palms of his hands. "He should have sold the Mustang."

The officer had his pad out again. "This might have been a mugging gone wrong, either way it's a homicide. I need your name, sir. I'm afraid you'll have to wait. I need to inform Major Crimes. They will want to talk to you for additional information. I'll wait with you." *Tibbett, isn't that the old murder/suicide case just reopened?*

"Dead, just like that." Connor needed a chair. He could think of no one to call. "Devon dead?" Connor heard someone asking, "What did you say?"

CHAPTER FORTY-ONE

THE NEXT MORNING, Damiano was too happy to stay in bed, so she surprised Matte by arriving at the office before him. The small victory was dashed when Matte appeared. "I'm running a check on Martin Heron. Turns out he's a lawyer, so he's no crazy. No record, oh yes, one citation for a traffic stop. Married eleven years with two children, but presently divorced. Are you listening, Pierre?"

"Every word. I see that the lethargy from the Ativan has worn off. Before I join in work, I must say that last night's dinner was succulent, all those good words. I don't usually eat fries, but those shoestring homemade fries were decadent. You saw I had a second helping. The whole meal and company were superb."

"We'll do a repeat. I'm going to live! The additional CT scan does worry me a bit. Now, let's deal with Heron."

"He didn't deny Hughes's story. He did say that his sister was very agitated, hinting that it was more than a broken promise. He said he feared his sister might have unwittingly driven Hughes to the Tibbetts that night of the killings."

"Pierre, I'll get in touch with Hughes and attempt to learn the name of the lawyer from Ottawa. He'll have a special reason for recalling the exact night of the official breakup with Stephanie Heron in the lobby of the Holiday Inn with his own wife up in their hotel room. It's better than fiction."

"Real life always is. I'll ask him to look through what belongings he kept of hers to see if there is a note with his name on it. He'll be more willing than Hughes, I think, for obvious reasons. If Hughes has nothing to hide, she might recall the lawyer's name. One way or another we'll find him."

Benoit Fortin, the officer who had assisted Connor Tibbett in the early morning hours in what was not a mugging, but a homicide, was no slouch. He had studied Police Technology at Cégep Gérald Godin and gone on to study Law and Criminology at the Université de Montréal. He was fluent in both languages and considered himself as a rising star. He had delayed Tibbett for a half hour at the hospital until he had all the additional information to hand in to Major Crimes. He also kept abreast of open cases, and the name Tibbett did not escape him. He'd check later to see which detectives were working the case and impress them with astute notes.

Tibbett caught on that the officer had made the connection to the open case. He set about to protect himself from suspicion. "Officer, my brother-in-law told us all what great surveillance the whole building boasted of having because of past problems with break-ins. You should get in touch with the super to release the CCTV video of the garage which will show my brother-in-law driving in slowly, and then falling out of his car. It will have me running over to help him and almost carrying him to his apartment."

"How come you were even in the garage, sir?"

"It was raining, and I knew I'd have a long wait. He needed the four grand, so I followed a car inside and waited for him. I knew I wouldn't miss his red Mustang. Initially, I had refused to lend him the money, but he told me he'd be in for a beatdown, not his first. I decided to give him the money. I knew he'd never be able to repay it, but he was family.

"I can't believe Devon's dead. As soon as his face changed color, I would have done CPR, but his ribs were broken, so I called for an ambulance. It was going to take an hour, minimum! That's worse than a Third World country. Now, he's dead. He doesn't have to worry about debts anymore. I'll never forgive myself for at first refusing to provide him with the money, and now it's too late. Emma's heart will be broken again. They had started seeing each other. I can't believe it. He'd be thirty-seven next month. How the fuck does this happen? Officer, can I leave? I'd like to be alone."

"Yes. The detectives working the case will contact you."

Connor walked out into persistent drizzle. "Will it all ever stop?" He thought of the agenda, his fingerprints, the broken lock and his left eyelid began to twitch. Connor's color returned when the officer allowed him to leave. The only other kindness ever afforded him by the police occurred the night of the murders. The detectives who were at the house took his clothes, checked his hands, his hair and took his prints. Seeing that he was in shock, they allowed him to sleep the night at the student housing complex with his friend Timothy Lang. He couldn't bear being in that house one more hour. Kindness didn't last. He was summoned the next day for more repeated tests. He remembered the term they used, GSR, particles that could be detected five days later. He was drilled about the missing weapon. Connor grimly realized that he'd moved from the person who found his parents, to their number one suspect.

For an intelligent man, he'd blundered from one thing to another without intention. Who hadn't confided in a sibling? Emma had told him way back that she and Devon weren't ready and didn't want children. He could have hurt Michael, but he kept Emma's secret that changed with time. Why did she memorialize confidences in that damn book like a teenager? Exaggerate a momentary burst of righteous anger for all the damage done by his father? That goddamn book had forced him to seek out Devon and bribe him for a few pages of rubbish. Earlier, Devon had caught him like a thief in the night. Once the detectives called him into the division, he could hear that Damiano saying he was the last person with Devon, implying the worst again. What were the chances they wouldn't find the agenda? Minimal.

Without realizing what he was doing, he'd walked back to Devon's car. He spotted the dark stains on the seats, almost smelled the blood. *That's Devon's blood. How could he die just like that! How?* Connor was edgy already, and the silence in the car unsettled him. He played with the audio menu on the Mustang's screen and caught Nikki Yanofsky's "Forget." *They won't forget about me either.* He drove home stone-faced.

CHAPTER FORTY-TWO

CONNOR SHOWERED AND shaved, waiting on the phone call he knew was coming. By two o'clock, the phone hadn't rung. He drove over to Emma's and waited for the boys. Just before three that afternoon, Terry bounded through the front door and stopped dead in his tracks, disappointed at not finding his father. That disappointment continued for Bobby and Michael. "Where's Dad?" Terry asked.

"He couldn't be here, so I'll drive you to see your mom and her new cast."

"Dad promised," Terry whined. "He broke his promise."

"He's not able to be here."

"We want to know why. He used to always pull this shit. I thought he had changed," Michael said angrily.

Connor steadied himself and ran his hand across his forehead. "Sit down, all of you. Please."

"We're all good on our feet. Dad split again. That's not new to us."

"Michael, shut up for a minute!" Blunt was the only way Connor knew. "Your father died early this morning."

"He's dead?" Michael shouted, his voice breaking. "How?"

"He had gambling debts, and…"

"He always had debts. We know."

"Well, the money that he gave to your mom was owed to loan sharks. Do you know what they are?"

"The goons who break your legs," Michael said knowingly.

"Or worse."

Terry and Bobby were crying openly like the boys they were. Michael was angry.

"I want to tell you the truth. He asked me for a loan. At first, I refused. Last night, I changed my mind. He had said he had some of the money and he thought they'd give him a few extra days. I drove to his place and waited for him in the building's garage because it

148

was raining. When he drove into the garage erratically, I knew right away there was something wrong. He fell out of his car before I got to him. He was injured. With difficulty I got him onto a couch in his apartment. He was okay …"

"But he wasn't okay!" Michael shouted again as though Connor was at fault.

"His condition worsened. I called 911 but was told it would take an hour for an ambulance to arrive, so I managed to get your dad to his car and rushed to the hospital. The doctors did what they could. I still can't believe it, so I know you can't either. I'm begging you all not to tell your mother now. This sad news can wait."

No one said anything. "Did you ever meet your grandfather?"

"A long time ago, when we were young. Why are you asking?" Michael wanted to know.

"I was just wondering who I could call?"

"You don't have to call anybody. He had us! Don't you get anything?"

Connor didn't say another word. It was hard on the boys.

Terry jumped in. He was still crying. "We have to tell Mom. She's the only one who'd know what to do. We can't just leave Dad alone at the hospital. That's not right."

"We can't trouble your mom now. We have to let the doctors perform an autopsy to determine the actual cause of death. They have to have evidence to find the loan sharks who killed Devon. Your mother needs another day. She's in no shape to deal with Devon's death. She had surgery yesterday, and they reset her tibia fracture."

"What will happen to us?" Terry asked, wiping his cheeks.

"I'll do the best I can."

"But you're not our father."

"No, I'm not, but I'm the best you're going to get. Now, I suggest you wipe away your tears and we head to the hospital."

The boys found their mother sitting in a large chair with her right leg elevated. Her mother's smile took them all in as they went to kiss her and hug her.

"Mom, no damage, I will be off the crutches tomorrow," Michael added.

"Wish I could say the same for me. Two orderlies lifted me to the chair. My throat is still raw, but it's wonderful to see you boys. I feel so much better just having you here. I was hoping Devon would be with you."

"He couldn't be here, Em."

Emma smiled ruefully. She looked at Connor, "Is this all too much for him? Is he pulling away?"

Three loud voices shouted, "NO!" Tears burst onto the young cheeks.

"What's happened?"

"Dad's dead. He died this morning, and he's all alone at the hospital!" Terry wailed. "I wasn't supposed to tell you, but it just came out."

Emma broke down, and her sons went to her. Connor stood alone.

CHAPTER FORTY-THREE

CONNOR WAITED ALONE while the boys comforted their mother and themselves. "I thought he was coming home to stay," Michael said. Bobby and Terry nodded their heads in agreement.

"I think he was," Emma said longingly. "You dad was never free of gambling. Way back, I thought I could change him, but most of us can't change."

"Who will take care of him at the hospital? We're all here."

Connor left the doorway and joined them. "Would you boys wait outside? I have some things to discuss with your mum." They wouldn't move. It was fortunate that Emma had the room to herself.

"Did he suffer?"

"Broken ribs are painful, but that's all he thought he had. That's why I helped him up to his place where he could rest and manage to sleep."

"What happened?"

"He started coughing up blood and gasping for air. The ambulance was going to take too long so I managed to get him into the car and I drove him to the Glen. I was told a rib had punctured his lung and he couldn't breathe. The doctor said he did his best."

"The money he gave me was part of the debt then?"

"That's why I went to his place to lend him four thousand. I didn't think they'd lay into him that night. I was hoping I'd have my money to him in time. It wasn't to be. His last name was Shore, right? Where do his parents live? He has a brother too."

"Toronto. His brother, I don't know."

"His father's name?"

"Richard, I think, or Phillip. I'm not sure."

"His father will have to pick up his personal belongings. I drove him in his car to the Glen, so I took what he had in his car back to his place. I left his keys there. The police will want access to his place and his phone and whatever. I'll give them that information, be the intermediary until his father arrives. You're not in any condition to deal with police. This is an additional blow for you, Em. I'm very sorry for everything."

"I can't think – Devon is gone… We were just beginning to really talk. There was a chance we might have…"

"Dad made us clean our rooms, and we didn't hate him anymore. He bought us food too," Bobby felt he had to add the salute to his father. "I think he even liked us. He was like a real dad."

"He helped me out bigtime, Mom. He was okay."

"Guys, I think your mom needs to rest now."

"No, I want the boys with me. I'm heartbroken. I always loved him, Connor."

"Here's some money for the cafeteria. Get something to eat. I'll be back later then. I didn't sleep last night, so I'll head home." Connor realized as he left that no one was listening to him. Driving, he often looked down at the passenger seat and saw what he had wanted to destroy since he was aware it contained his outburst. What to do with it was the question. The boys knew Devon had taken the agenda, but with their father dying, would they remember?

He had to move quickly. The boys were giving him short shrift as they saw to their mother, but they would expect him to be back to drive them home. He'd figured out where to hide the agenda, but that meant he had to go to the house. The Metro supermarket was first on the list. He picked up potatoes and steaks and milk. He drove to Broadview, praying that the hidden house key hadn't been moved. Luck was with him, and he entered the house quietly, stored the food, and took out the agenda he had hidden in the food bag. He found the basket of recipe books and stowed it in the pile. The tiny lock was gone. He hoped Devon's death would diminish any recollection of the damned book.

He still was beyond anger that a little insignificant, cheap copybook could be his undoing. Burning the damned thing was the way to go, but he didn't dare. He'd found his parents, he'd been with Devon when he died, and the smell and proof of him were in the infernal book. With no nefarious intent on his part, a simple outburst, long coming, could now seal his fate. He felt guilty enough that he had wasted precious minutes arguing with Devon about the damn thing, minutes that might have saved Devon's life. No one would ever know that, and he certainly would never reveal it. It was the damning book, no, it was Emma, that could ruin his life.

Connor would never trust her again. When she recovered, and if he was still a free man, knowing that she'd practically turned in her own brother bore consequences. Emma would be dead to him forever. Those actions were intended for the future. Right now, he needed a shower, a change of clothes and a rush back to the hospital. Timothy was set to arrive tomorrow, and to his surprise, Connor longed to see him, to hold him. He needed someone who loved him. The kids had made their choice clear. After he had sent Timothy packing and after the agenda, Connor knew exactly the utter loneliness of being abandoned, so, for now, he'd play the good brother and make the attempt to work his way back into the family.

The boys were circled around their mother, and he was intruding again. To his surprise, Emma said she needed a few minutes with Connor.

"We're right out in the hall, Mom, if you need us," Michael said possessively.

"Connor, the nurses told me you stayed with me for two nights and days."

"I didn't want you to be alone or frightened."

"Thank you." He saw the tears in her eyes and tried not to smile. "They want to release me home or to rehab. At home, I can have a nurse from the CLSC drop in to see me a few times a week. The boys want me home, and they could fix me up with a bed. I needed to ask what you thought was best. I realize you've missed work and can't continue to be here every day."

"Well, I'd ask them to send you to the Lakeshore Hospital for a few days of rehab. They can get you up and help you walk with crutches and then go home."

"That's exactly what I'll do. Can I ask you again, did Devon suffer? You can tell me now."

"He was in a shitload of pain, but he really thought it was just the ribs. He was taken by surprise, as was I, when things turned so quickly."

"At least, you were there. He didn't die alone."

"Cold comfort to him now. Don't cry, Em. You have to think of yourself now." He reached into his pocket and handed her the four thousand. "I hope this helps."

Emma struggled with her thoughts. "Maybe I misjudged you, Connor."

He produced his best boyish smile, bent over and kissed his sister.

CHAPTER FORTY-FOUR

MARTIN HERON'S CALL was the first of three. "Detective Damiano."

"Martin Heron, Detective. I've gone through all six boxes and I cannot find a single name. I didn't realize how intelligent my sister was. I found the beginnings of a book of satire she had written, and I found myself laughing out loud in spite of the circumstances. Her notes are even interesting. I was suddenly proud of her. I'm so glad I kept this material. I'm beginning to feel I shouldn't have bothered you.

"My sister died in an accident. No one pushed her. I guess no one pushed me on the escalator. I just experienced some sort of panic attack."

"Have you had others?"

Martin paused. He did not want the detective thinking he was a nutcase. "No. I've been nervous at times, but nothing close to this occasion. Then again, I don't make it a habit of falling down escalators."

"So, you're normal like the rest of us."

"I'm afraid so."

"Have you still concerns about your fall, or the deaths of the Tibbetts?"

"Something was off with Steph, but I have no sure idea what. We were never close, as I've said, so I could be completely off the mark. To answer your question – I have no plausible doubts."

Damiano put her phone down. But within seconds, her phone rang and she picked it up before she saw Matte signal to her. "Detective Damiano."

"This is Doctor Zagan, Detective."

"So, you've seen the results."

"Yes, I have Detective, but I am not convinced. I think we may have caught this cancer in its incipient stages. I've scheduled another CT scan."

Damiano threw her head back, "Fine, but I know there is nothing. I won't endure that stress again."

"I like to be conclusive. You're a relatively young woman."

"Thank you for the good care." She wanted to throw her phone against the wall. "Pierre, Zagan is still not certain I don't have lung cancer!"

"He's being cautious."

"I don't care. There is no cancer in my lungs! He'll end up causing me to have a stroke."

"Try to calm down. I tend to agree, but humor him and take another scan."

"Nothing ever ends. What does?"

"Death."

"It was a general question – no need to be morbid."

"Truth is morbid."

"I thought truth was beauty."

"Ah, Keats' version, but truth is anything laid bare of its extremities, standing alone as an isolate. Hard to bear for most of us."

"True, but stop, we're off topic, Pierre. I have to call Sandra Hughes."

"An Officer Fortin has information connected to our case. I told him to be here at eleven."

"That's something. I put us on speakerphone for Hughes." Damiano checked the number and called. "Detective Damiano here."

"Yes?"

"I have further questions."

"I sense that Steph's brother Martin has contacted you. It's funny. Steph and I were best friends, an old term, for ten years, and she might have given her brother ten minutes of air time. Now, he's front and center with information about her. What's the question?" Her tone was not amused.

"Do you recall the name of the man who broke his promise to her?"

"Kenneth. I saw a photo of him once. He was a short man, ergo, not a Ken."

"A last name?"

"The first name that comes to mind is Moore, but that sounds too much like paint. Stuart? I'm not sure at all."

"He was a lawyer though?"

"I recall that. Constitutional law. Steph liked that. Since we last spoke, I've done some thinking about her. I used to feel sorry for her and her heartbreaks. I'd blame her for her bad choices. But now, I realize that love isn't something anyone can control. She fell in love and she pursued it and bore the scars of failures. We all make fools of ourselves for love. She refused to settle, though many do. I almost envy her, almost. The Greeks were more tolerant of errant love and lovers."

"Do you have more to tell us of him?"

"Only that Steph drove out from Montreal West to have another go at Kenneth who was still at the hotel. She surprised me. We parked behind the hotel, and I spent many minutes talking her out of the idea. She was very upset, mostly because she wasn't deeply in love. He was the lover, and he'd chucked her and his promise. And, that was not the night of the murders. I've checked."

"We'd like to reach this lawyer. He would surely recall the dates. The situation is not exactly usual."

"Good luck, then."

"Rest assured we will contact you."

Sandra tightened her grip on the phone long after the call ended.

Matte was already searching for a Kenneth somebody in constitutional law in Ottawa.

Damiano sat musing. "It's strange. When have we dealt with truthful suspects? They all hold back or lie outright. Hughes could have said she couldn't recall this lawyer's name or his particular law practice. No one could have held her to account, yet she was forthright. Either she has nothing to hide or she is very confident. We have to discover which."

A colleague leaned into the murder room. "There's an Officer Fortin waiting to see you."

CHAPTER FORTY-FIVE

"Pierre, do you want to continue with the lawyer or stay with me?"

"Let's see what this Fortin has, and then I'll decide."

Fortin was a tall, slim young man with a studious, self-assured look about him. His eyes were small and eager. Certainly, not someone who'd gnaw at his lower lip, or smile easily. There was a '*make way, I'm coming through*' demeanor that Damiano didn't like. She noticed both folders; he came prepared.

She waved Fortin into the murder room. "Detective Damiano."

"Matte, please sit."

"Thank you, Officer Benoit Fortin." He carefully moved their files to one side to make room for his own.

Damiano opened her mouth, but Matte gave her a *no* signal.

"Detectives, I worked on my own time to be certain I have my notes in order. I know you are working the Tibbett case. What I have is Connor Tibbett with his ex-brother-in-law Devon Shore. Shore was a gambler who borrowed from loan sharks or bookies. A day and a half ago, he was beaten with a crowbar for an outstanding debt. Shore thought all he had suffered were broken ribs. Unfortunately, one of the ribs had punctured his lung.

"Let me go back a bit. Earlier that afternoon, Shore was at Emma Tibbett's home where he had helped his ex with the boys. I presume you heard that Emma Tibbett was the victim of a hit-and-run and was seriously injured. Shore had stepped in and helped his estranged sons. So, apparently the money he gave Emma Tibbett was owed to his debtors. Connor Tibbett was at the house as well. Shore asked him for a loan, Tibbett refused at first. The gambling had gone on for years, as well as beatdowns. Shore, according to Tibbett, said he had two thousand and he thought the sharks would give him a couple of days."

Damiano and Matte were thinking the same thing. What was Connor Tibbett doing at his sister's house?

Fortin went on. "Tibbett had a change of heart and drove to Shore's place to lend him the money. I have the footage with me. Shore finished work at three a.m. Tibbett waited in the rain. He finally decided to get into the garage, also on the footage I have, and wait for him there. You will see Shore drive his red Mustang very slowly and unsurely into the garage. Tibbett ran to him, but not before he fell out of the car. He carried him to his apartment. I have no footage of inside the apartment itself. Tibbett says he lifted Shore to the sofa. Shore thought he had broken ribs, nothing worse. Then things turned. Shore quite suddenly couldn't breathe.

"Tibbett called for an ambulance but was told there would be a delay, so he carried him back down to his car. I have footage of that, and confirmation that he did call for an ambulance. He was speeding on his way to the Glen, which is why I pulled him over. When I realized what was happening, I escorted them to the hospital. Shore died minutes after arrival. Tibbett was shaken, I can attest to that. He stood looking at a bank envelope stuffed with money. I waited with Tibbett until he was handed Shore's personal belongings.

"I've learned that the autopsy will be performed tomorrow, but the on-site physician said preliminary examination concurs with the theory Tibbett gave me." Fortin finished with a flush of success across his cheeks. "I don't know if this helps at all, but it is a connection, and I felt you'd want to have it."

Damiano rose above her first impressions and said, "Yes, this information is definitely an addition to our investigation. Good work, Matte, and I appreciate it."

Fortin's hunger was back. "Would you like me to follow up on any of this? On my own time, of course. I have heard of your reputation, and I'm striving to aim high myself."

While Damiano was swallowing a laugh, Matte helped her out. "If we think of anything, we will contact you, Officer Fortin. Leave a number with us."

Fortin tried to hide his disappointment. He handed his card to Matte. "Well, I wish you a good day."

His formality drew a squeak from Damiano that Matte hid with a cough. Fortin disappeared. "Give the kid a break. I thought you were trying to be a better person."

"There are limits, and he was one of them."

CHAPTER FORTY-SIX

MATTE HAD HIS PHONE in his hand to contact Kenneth Morrison when Damiano raised her arm. "We need a few minutes. We are both going in circles. Doctor Zagan is not convinced I don't have lung cancer, and I believe he will haunt me about nothing for months. Like our case. Where are we? The dentist didn't need to murder the Tibbetts, and he will probably come up with the proof. Emma Tibbett is, we suspect, holding back, but we can't question her because she's still in the hospital. She was the victim of a hit-and-run that has nothing whatsoever to do with our case. The brother-in-law appears, he might have helped us, but he's dead, the victim of a manslaughter. Bookies don't intentionally kill their pigeons; they drain them dry. Connor Tibbett, our best suspect, has secrets he never has to reveal, courtesy of the accidents. Did he know his father meant to change his will, and did he reveal anything to his sister? Did he take the gun? He found his parents, but he lived there, for God's sake.

"For the icing on the cake, you're about to contact a lawyer who dumped Hughes's best friend to get our dates straight. We're basing our investigation all on the concern of a brother who rarely saw his sister, suffers from panic attacks, and thinks maybe his sister drove Hughes to the Tibbetts' house unwittingly the night of the murder. Hughes has been nothing but truthful. She didn't have to give us this Kenneth. We'd have no way of getting it. According to Hughes herself, she'd only commit a perfect murder, but all she came up with was Woody Allen's magic dust.

"Who chose this bloody case? Oh wait, you did. We both need a shrink".

"Hold your horses, as my grandmother would say. On the cancer issue, I think you're healthy, but you'll take the CT scan on a niggling suspicion that just maybe Zagan is right. Concerning our case, we knew it's been investigated twice, it wasn't going to be an easy solve.

I will call the hospital after Morrison, just maybe, we can interview Emma Tibbett. Sandra Hughes is a smart woman who might just be toying with us."

"Or, telling us the truth. I'll call the Glen. Kenneth is yours. To give you space, I'll make the call from my office."

Matte called as soon as Damiano closed the door.

"Hewitt, Levins & Morrison."

"Kenneth Morrison."

"I'll connect you." The voice was pleasant and mature.

"Kenneth Morrison's office. How may I help you?'

"I'd like to speak with him."

"Have you a telephone appointment?"

"No, I don't."

"He's busy with clients at the moment. May I have your name…"

"I am Detective Pierre Matte, of Major Crimes in Montreal. Please put the call through."

"I, well…"

"I'm waiting."

"Yes, just a moment."

"Kenneth Morrison speaking."

"Detective Matte, Mr. Morrison. Are you the man who was once involved with Stephanie Heron?"

There was a nervous pause, but a lawyer knows to offer nothing up. "Yes."

"Sir, I just need verification of dates that you last met with her at the Holiday Inn."

Now there was a touch of impatience. "You mean ten years ago?"

"Yes. I realize you'd have to check your calendar for this, but I assume you might remember the actual days of the week because of the nature of the embarrassing event."

"Memory is part and parcel of my work. It was a Tuesday and Wednesday."

Matte could sense Morrison's tension.

"What is all this concerning?"

"The murders we are investigating were committed the following night."

"You mean that couple in the West Island?"

"I do."

"Detective, I had nothing to do with that tragedy. You've heard the story of the lobby." Morrison rapped a fist against his forehead. *Why say that at all?*

"I have."

"I was a jerk."

"Did you ever speak with Ms. Heron after the event?"

"Twice."

"Did she seem nervous, distraught?"

"Yes."

"Did she reveal something other than your past relationship?"

"Steph had her own dark periods. I have mine. That was something we shared, but they passed. I knew her for thirteen years, but she was especially edgy and angry."

"You didn't enquire?"

"I knew I was responsible, but I just wanted out. There was nothing more for either one of us. Then she was killed, and she has left me with lifelong remorse and guilt and a deadening shame."

"That will be all, Mr. Morrison."

Morrison clicked off. He broke a pen in half, smearing ink on both his hands. He threw the pieces against the wall. *Too late, Steph. Too friggin' late for apologies.*

CHAPTER FORTY-SEVEN

WHEN DAMIANO RETURNED to the murder room, she saw from Matte's face he didn't have much.

"Hughes and Heron were together Tuesday and Wednesday, apparently, but I have no information where they were on the Thursday night."

"Doesn't mean they weren't together, Pierre."

"We're reaching again, just as you said."

"Look, we will have Connor Tibbett in the interrogation room, mark my words, but we still need more on him. What was he doing at his sister's house the same time Shore was there? What's between sister and brother, and what are they hiding? With Hughes, we're still searching. Pierre, call down to fraud, see where they are on the Shore case. Did they find anything for us?"

Matte was on the phone for ten minutes. "Lucky buggers! Shore wasn't a big-time gambler, mostly he kept it to a ten-thousand-dollar debt. Had the bookie's number in his phone log, called him twice that night. Turns out the bookie uses a bouncer for his muscle. The fellow can't believe he actually killed Shore. He was just due for a rough-up. Now the bouncer and bookie are facing manslaughter charges. They found nothing unexpected in the apartment. Officer Fortin got in touch with them as well. Emile Boucher said they found him helpful."

"So, they accepted Tibbett's account because that's all they had, really?"

"Boucher is thorough. He said the facts and video footage support Tibbett's account."

"I'll call the hospital. Emma Tibbett might be able to see us now." Damiano spoke to a nurse for a few minutes. "We need no more than fifteen minutes, and the need is urgent. Yes, we'll be there in an hour."

"Tibbett is being discharged tomorrow at noon. She was slated to go to Lakeshore General Hospital, but they can't take her for rehab.

Lachine General would, but she chose to rehab at home for her children's sake. The CLSC is involved. That's why I chose to see her today. Tomorrow her home will be a madhouse."

"Fine, Toni, let's get going then, and when she is settled, we'll have a second round of questioning."

Once en route, Damiano said, "I'm going to try the gentle approach."

"You?"

"I can do gentle. If you see me failing, take over."

Tibbett was alone, with the exception of her neighbor patient who was sound asleep.

Matte and Damiano walked in quietly. Tibbett was sitting propped up in a large chair. "We are glad to see you on the mend. You've come through a rough time. We won't take up too much of your time. We came today because tomorrow will be a busy and stressful one for you."

Tibbett did her best not to appear startled, and pulled the blue hospital gown across her good leg. "I'm happy to be out of here, but stressed about the logistics of being home."

Damiano gave Matte a *see* look that Tibbett missed. "Look, Emma, may I call you Emma?"

"Sure." Tibbett wasn't fooled, but she could play the game.

"Your parents, good or bad people, or just your average couple, were gunned down. I would think you and your brother would want to help. We speak for them, as for any victims. We're pretty good cops and we accept that people always hold back, but there comes a time for truth. You are not a suspect. We are interested in the weapon. How old was your brother at the time?"

"Twenty-two."

"That's young to come upon such a tragedy. He was probably in shock, didn't fully realize what he was doing. He may have taken the weapon to save your parents the scandal. We do think he took the gun." Damiano's approach firmed up.

"You don't know that for certain. I don't know that at all."

"If it was a professional hit, the weapon used would be non-traceable and dropped at the scene. Like Michael did in *The Godfather*, you saw the film, of course?"

"Four times. The killer could also be anyone with a grudge."

"True. Obstruction of justice is a serious matter, a felony actually. I believe you don't know. I'm not suggesting you are obstructing, but

I am telling you to give us what you might have that will help us to put some closure on the tragedy, because that's what it is, a tragedy."

Now that Devon was gone, Connor was all she had. He'd been generous and attentive. How could she turn on her brother? Her fears were still doubtful, she didn't know anything for sure. "I have to think about this."

"I trust that you will, Emma. We are not the enemy."

Emma thought of the recent kindness of Connor, but the other fears were still there. Her leg was instantly hot and burning, and her shoulders ached. There had to be some kind of closure. She couldn't go on blocking out the fears she harbored.

CHAPTER-FORTY-EIGHT

SANDRA HUGHES WAS NOT a woman easily riled, but once she was, she fought back, not unlike a pit bull. Finding Martin Heron was easy. No one could hide, she thought. He answered tentatively, so she knew he had caller ID. "Martin, it's Sandra Hughes. We spoke a while ago." Hughes could detect the reticence at the other end of the phone.

"Yes, I recall."

"I know you have contacted the police."

"I, I may have overstepped."

"That's putting it mildly. You told the police that Steph may have, what word did you use, oh yes, *unwittingly* driven me to the Tibbetts to murder them."

"I, I didn't mean it to come out so harshly."

"Oh, you did, Martin, you did."

"I'm…"

"What Martin?"

"I'm…"

"It's too late for sorry, so it must mean you're scared. Are you scared, Martin? Do you know what it means to have a best friend?"

"I…"

"For God's sake listen. For ten years, Steph was the best friend I ever had. We trusted one another with our secrets, we wished the best for each other, and we acted on those feelings. Steph was a great support to me during the difficult, sad time James and I endured. I, in turn, helped her through the troubled times of her life. We leaned on one another.

"I would *never* betray her trust by using her to cover up a crime, a murder no less. I'd be responsible for making her an accessory after the fact. How dare you even suppose I would do such a thing! How dare you!"

"All I recall is that Steph was distraught, highly distraught."

"I stupidly related the story of the Holiday Inn to the police; a story Steph wouldn't have wanted you to know. There was a second part that I will not disclose because Steph wouldn't have shared it with you."

"Well, I didn't know," was his petulant reply.

"No, you wouldn't. You didn't know your sister. Are you having qualms of conscience now that you can't fix things between you? I know some of your nasty stories; Steph shared them with me. I often said you two should be friends. She'd say, 'Martin is a mean, miserable human being. We'll never be friends.' Are you still there, Martin?"

"There are two sides to any story." He sounded like a twelve-year-old.

"I have no interest in your side. You're no friend of mine."

"I, I am…"

"Too late. Watch your step, Martin," she said ominously. "After all, you did insinuate to the police I might be a murderer, didn't you? You intrusive, insignificant weakling!" Sandra smiled wickedly. *He deserved that.*

Martin stepped back too quickly onto the burgundy floral throw rug that he'd meant to buy under-padding for and never got around to. He tottered awkwardly, prevented a fall, but stubbed his little toe into the leg of the glass coffee table and yelped. "I've broken my toe!" He began hopping dangerously on one foot. His balance had never been good, and he was grateful he landed on the side of an upholstered chair. He pulled himself upright and sat alone, grabbing his foot and realizing Hughes had cut the connection.

"Would a normal woman talk to me like this, or hang up on me?" Dangerous and wicked people do not endanger us as much as stupid people who deceive themselves. Martin believed he was under siege, and never gave a thought to the reality that he had begun the ugly situation. "Let me think. I can't go back to the police, they might agree with her, but what I can do is tail her." Like Hamlet, he caught himself thinking, *the tail is the thing wherein I'll catch the bitch.* "Then I go to the police with evidence.

"I have to plan this very carefully. Sandra wouldn't remember me. We barely nodded to one another at the funeral. She was weeping, so of course, the whole day was a blur. She doesn't know my car. I'll wear my contacts, and I'll park in different places. Some days, I'll walk carrying brown bags like a new neighbor." A nervous twitch shook his whole body. "What if she spots me?

"I run, but I look like the nutcase she thinks I am. Well, I just can't let that happen." His words were braver than he felt. He rose from the chair, and for one second forgot his toe, and nearly fell. "Shoot! What am I going to do? I can't even walk! Worse, what if she kills me, and the police find me on her street. She pleads self-defense. I can't worry about that now. I have to take care of my toe. Walk first, plan carefully. One thing is for certain, she is not free of me! No one takes me for a fool.

"What were her exact words? 'Watch your step.' Why not the usual *your back*? Because she knew about the escalator? She knew I had been pushed!"

CHAPTER FORTY-NINE

THE FOLLOWING DAY WAS busy for Detective Damiano and Connor Tibbett. Doctor Zagan had set up the CT scan at St. Mary's Hospital, a locale easier to reach than the General. She didn't bother telling Jeff and Pierre. She found parking a few blocks from the hospital and since walking was slow, she jogged. Like some record, she was done in less than forty minutes and driving back to the division.

Connor Tibbett was up at five, working and trying to catch up on the files he had neglected. At nine, he was in the car driving to the West Island to meet a woman from the CLSC who promised to bring equipment his sister would need at the house. They both arrived at the same time. Connor carried the walker and the crutches into the house. "No, you don't have to carry anything, Mrs. Dupont. That's for me to do." An elevated toilet seat was next and a bench for the hand scrubs, along with something called a grabber. Dupont also had brought Depends. "I can't see my sister in diapers."

"You never know, accidents happen," Dupont said sagely. "Now I have another patient to see. Tell your sister I'll be here from nine to eleven, three days a week. I see you've requested someone for the other two days. I'm free, but that's private, and the fee is twenty dollars an hour."

Connor had brought ready cash.

"Thank you, Mr. Tibbett. This helps with the rising prices of everything. I'm never late."

Connor saw Dupont to the door, turned back and hunted down sheets and pillows for the hospital bed that arrived before Dupont. He'd rented the bed for a month. "Oh shit, the milk." He rushed outside to get the six two-liter cartons that were still in his trunk. "The boys drink this like water. Thank God, the milk is still cold." He transferred some food to the extra fridge in the basement.

The recipe basket was beside the fridge. He saw the slim spine of the agenda. He could take it now, destroy it and be rid of the damn thing. Terry knew Devon had it. He'd figured that out. Destroying it meant digging himself further into the whole mess. Showing Emma that he loved her, sacrificing himself and his time for her, not to mention the money, should convince her to get rid of his angry words that were never meant for other ears. He'd even told her he'd pick her up and drive her home. All of this work had to count for something. He left the agenda where it was.

Emma was trying to pack up her things when the phone rang. "Emma, this is Phillip Shore. Do you have some time to talk? The medical staff haven't told me much. A physician indicated how Devon died, but not why he died. I need as much information as I can find. It's been very difficult for me and the family back in Toronto."

Emma began to weep. A nurse went to her. Emma said, "I have to take this call. I'm alright."

"Are you still there?"

"Yes, Phillip. I loved Devon."

"He was loved here too. A black sheep is loved perhaps more because he needs help."

"I have to tell you I'm in the hospital…"

When she finished, Phillip broke in. "I am so sorry. I had no way of knowing."

Between the sobs, "Phillip, before my accident, Devon came to see me with money for child support, money he owed. We had dinner together. And," Emma wept louder, "I fell for him again. After the accident, and I was here in the hospital, Devon took over. Bought food, stayed with the boys, got them to clean their rooms to surprise me. The boys held a deep resentment for not having a father with them. Within one day, he won them over. When they learned of his death, they were devastated and they told me what he had done for them. He was trying to change, and I think he wanted to come back to his family. I had such hope for a second chance. Time wasn't on his side." Emma could hear Phillip attempt to gather himself.

"I didn't learn of this, but I am comforted to hear he was making an effort. He wasn't a bad son, but he broke our hearts many times over the years. Even his gambling addiction wasn't massive, small time really. He'd promise his mother he'd be home for Christmas, but he never made it. I understand your brother was with him the night he died."

"Connor had gone to his apartment to lend him the money he owed. He waited for him to come home after work. Devon had some cash, and he thought the bookie would give him a few days to secure the rest. But the people he owed, loan sharks, I guess, had gotten to Devon, but he managed to drive home wounded. Connor carried and dragged him up to his apartment. Devon said it was just broken ribs, but suddenly he couldn't breathe. Connor drove him to the Glen Hospital because the minimum was an hour delay for an ambulance. Connor was shaken, but he said Devon died so suddenly he didn't have time to be afraid. He didn't die alone, Phillip."

"I…I'm glad of that. How much did he still owe?"

"Four thousand."

"That's all his life was worth to these bookies. As I said, Devon had big ideas, but my son was small time."

"He wasn't to me or his sons, three beautiful sons."

"I'll be in Montreal for another four days. They will release Devon's body, perhaps tomorrow, and I have made the plans for his cremation at Rideau Funeral Home. I'll move out to the West Island to avoid the city traffic on my way back to Toronto. May I drive over to meet the boys? It's been so long since I last saw them."

"That's a lovely idea. Your visit will help them accept their father's sudden death. They're still in shock. You'll have to accept me as I am, leg cast and anything remotely comfortable. It's been difficult."

"Of course, Emma. This visit will help me too. I didn't fool myself about Devon. He'd bounce around, and I expected that. Broke our hearts, and yours, but I never thought I'd lose my son. We all lost Devon so suddenly. There was much left unsaid, because I always thought we'd have time. That he would come to his senses. I'm so glad to hear he was trying to change his life."

"How about tomorrow night after dinner, at seven thirty. The boys have school, so it won't be a long visit."

"You've made me very happy. His mother wants his ashes with us. It's time Devon came home."

"I understand."

CHAPTER FIFTY

CONNOR TIBBETT WORKED late into the night, and in the morning, he had driven to the Sacred Heart Hospital to take Emma home. He hoped to make use of the time he had with her to gently force her to destroy the damaging words in her bloody book. Timothy was arriving, he hoped by six. Connor had changed the sheets, cleared his old dresser and emptied a closet. As far as Emma was concerned, he had pushed the passenger seat forward and brought a pillow for the back seat. He parked around the corner from the hospital and went to fetch her.

The staff was so eager to free the bed that Emma was already in a wheelchair with one leg raised, and her belongings in a plastic bag on her knee. "Wow! You're all set."

"I think I was kind of rushed, but I didn't mind. I want to go home. It seems like a year. I know I was lucky, and I will remember my second chance for the rest of my life. I never really understood how a life can be lost in seconds, and I will never take it for granted again."

Connor related to Emma at length what he had done for her and paid for. "I was glad to do all of it, Em. We only have each other. Timothy is coming back, because we both want to make a go of it. I called him. I was actually lonely and tired." He was about to begin his attempt to right things, but Emma cut in.

"Phillip Shore called me last night."

"Devon's father?"

"I was taken aback, but he is so sad and lonely in Montreal, waiting to have Devon's body released and then cremated that I actually welcomed his call. It helped me. I'm still numb and grieving. I always loved Devon, even after he left us. I always hoped… and now it's all over before it began. I know you could be just as easily cremating my body. Survivor's guilt is real, I can tell you."

"I hear you. I never thought I needed anyone. Needing was weak, and I blew up relationships. I was selfish, and I used people, but I want Timothy and I to work this time."

"Phillip is coming to see the boys tonight."

"Can you manage that, Em? You're just home. You need to be very careful."

"I think his presence will do us all good. I know I'll see something of Devon in him. He should see his grandsons, and they him."

"Maybe you're right."

"It feels right. I can never thank you for all you've done, Connor."

"Yeah, you can."

"How? I forgot to tell you the detectives, both of them, came to talk to me earlier."

"In the hospital?"

"Yes. They were very kind. I knew it was a planned approach to soften me up."

Connor began to panic. Though it was April, he was sweating. With the CLSC woman coming at two-thirty, Shore tonight, when was he going to have a chance to convince Emma to give him the agenda? "We have a few minutes before we reach Broadview. Please hear me out. These detectives, I'm assuming, have one dangling suspect, me. I've read they have closed cases without a body. Here, they need the gun, or maybe not. I trusted you when I opened up. I made myself sound worse than I was. I was in shock. I couldn't move. Dad had that spongy blood around his nose and mouth. It wasn't that I refused to help – Christ, I couldn't move. The scene was like slow motion on steroids. Sounds like a contradiction, but it isn't.

"The police tested me, took my clothes, questioned me for two hours in the room with Mom and Dad. One second, I didn't care for them, the next, I was gagging and I vomited. You can't give them the agenda, that's all they need to arrest me. You have to hang with family. Mom and Dad are long gone. Let them be in peace."

"Is the agenda the reason you've been so good to me?"

Connor sighed loudly. "If it were, I would have left you alone in the hospital, saved money and taken the opportunity to tear your house apart till I found the agenda and destroyed it."

"I'm sorry, Connor. I won't do anything till we can sit down to-gether."

"I've earned that much. I've read up on Detective Damiano and

Detective Matte. They were the detectives that solved the sixty-four-year-old case a year and a half ago. There was a lot of congratulatory publicity for them. They have their teeth sunk into this one. It isn't just a case reread. They want to close the case. I'm in their sights. They can't fail as I see things. They're in it for solutions, for their reputations. There's politics involved. This is my life they are delving into. I need you on my side. I won't bother you, Em, till we talk together. You need peace and rest where you can find them.

"Here we are. Stay put while I fetch the crutches from the house. I hope they are padded as they promised. Be back in a jiffy."

Emma was upset, but did her best to hide her rising fear.

"Here they are, Mom, and padded! Let me ease you out by your legs. Then you grab my shoulders until you grab hold of the crutches. Okay?"

"I'll do my best."

"Good! There, you've done a great job, Em. You've lost weight. You look very good for someone who's been through surgery and a broken tibia. Really, you look good, sis. Let's go in by the side door and avoid the stairs."

Emma was quite capable of helping herself and her confidence grew. Once they were in the kitchen, she exclaimed, "Everything looks so clean."

"You can thank Devon for that. The boys' rooms are impeccable. He had them going."

"You all pitched in." Emma had tears in her eyes.

"Time for smiles."

"You're right."

"Go up to my room and take the agenda. It should be on the vanity."

"You mean it?"

"I do."

"Thanks, Em." Connor ran up the stairs, knowing he wouldn't find anything. He went to the closet and sent a silent thanks to Devon who had carefully replaced all the boxes. "I can't find it!" He came back down. "Em. One day, I asked Terry where it was and he said it was hidden. I'd forgotten. You were protected on all sides, you see."

"So, you wanted it."

"Just to see what you'd written, not to grab it. You're right, we have to talk. There is more at risk than my life alone. But right now, I'm glad you're home, you survived, and you will have the boys who love you. Don't overdo it with Devon's father. You need your rest. All in all, it's been a busy day for you."

Why can't I trust my own brother? Her fear of Connor had never left her. Her breathing slowed to an even rhythm only when Connor drove home.

CHAPTER FIFTY-ONE

MARTIN HERON HAD PUT in a full day tailing Sandra Hughes. He was pleased with himself that he'd chosen a jacket instead of the usual sweater that might too easily betray him. His colored contacts were additional camouflage. His normal brown eyes were now deep blue. He sat in his gray Corolla on Seigniory Avenue in front of one of the four Southwest One apartments. The large complex of apartments, garden homes, and townhouses was built in the British square style surrounded by attractive flower beds and shade trees. The many trucks parked on the street were a sign of ongoing apartment renovations.

Martin was tired. He was prepared to wait till eleven that night, but finally decided to leave by seven if Hughes didn't surface again. His back ached, he hadn't brought enough water and the two egg sandwiches were long gone. Worst of all, his bladder was about to burst. He'd see to the necessary changes for tomorrow's stalking of Hughes. A half hour was all he could make. He started the car and drove to the Harvey's restaurant on St. Charles Boulevard. On arrival, he headed straight for the washroom, not caring that the floor was sticky and both taps were dripping. He rushed past the counter, hurried out to his car and drove home.

He'd followed Hughes to the Metro supermarket in Pointe Claire Shopping Center and then to the pharmacy. From there, to the Marché de l'Ouest in Dollard-des-Ormeaux. There he dared to enter the Marché to follow her, from a safe distance, behind an older couple. He envied her purchase of cheese at Cavallaro, and could taste the aged Gruyère and thinly sliced Emmental. Then, she picked up a baguette from the Première Moisson bakery. His mouth stopped watering when she finally left.

Martin wasn't master of many trades, but he could drive. He knew the city, where to speed, where to be careful. His whole life, he had never received a ticket, just that one he never counted. He tailed Hughes down the Decarie Expressway, exited at Queen Mary and drove along Côte-des-Neiges until she turned into the iconic cemetery. She took a right past the main monument and a right again and stopped. A few feet from the narrow road, she stopped in front of a black monument. With a pail and rags she had taken from the car, she went about cleaning the stone. With the shears she brought with her, she set about clipping the grass. Kissing the monument, she collected her stuff and drove slowly away.

I must find out the name on that monument.

Hughes didn't leave the cemetery. She slowly drove along a narrow asphalt road and pulled over. Out came the pail and rags as she walked past three monuments and stopped in front of a brass plaque. Martin knew where Hughes was now. A sliver of guilt cut across Martin's heart. He hadn't been to his sister's grave since her funeral. Once Hughes was done, she placed the rags and pail in the trunk of her car and took out a bouquet of yellow roses. *How did she manage those without me noticing?* She kissed the cold brass, stood silent in prayer or thought, before she placed the roses at the foot of the monument. Hughes seemed reluctant to leave. Finally, slowly, she turned and went back to her car. Martin followed her back to the West Island.

Hughes walked to the dumpster that lay outside the right garage entrance of her apartment complex. She looked both ways before tossing a white garbage bag into the dumpster. He'd seen it all! He had to retrieve the bag, he had to. He had no other choice. When Hughes had gone, he crossed the street, walked over to the dumpster, looked around and took a deep breath. He saw the bag, but he was forced to jump to grab it, painfully striking his knee on the side of the dumpster. He limped over to his car and slammed the door. Goddamn knee throbbed with stabbing pain. "Great. Just great!"

He would check the bag at home. But curiosity got the better of him. He tore open the plastic bag. What if he, Martin Heron, had discovered evidence of the unsolved murder? What if Hughes…? He caught himself from going too far. Greedily he examined his find. What the…? Dirty white paper towels. For this he wounded himself. For this he wasted a whole day. He threw the waste on the passenger seat and dropped his head in despair.

He jumped at the angry rap on the window. Hughes was standing there. He didn't need anyone to tell him she was fuming. *Fuck!*

"Get out of the car! Now!"

He started the car and rolled down the window. "What?"

"Get out of the car, Martin."

What choice did he have? He got out and stood sheepishly.

"I was expecting something of the sort, but nothing this idiotic and dumb," Hughes said angrily and loudly. "Everywhere I went today, I've recorded you. This last bit is the jackpot."

"You set me up," Martin shot back, gathering what small courage he felt.

"Didn't have to. You did all the work yourself. I'll have you charged with stalking."

"You can't do that! Somebody pushed me on the escalator. I could have died."

"What are you talking about?"

"At Ogilvy's, the escalator. I could have died."

"You need help, Martin. Yes, I remember now, Steph once told me you had some sort of breakdown. You're having another episode. Maybe a stalking charge will shake some sense into you."

"Please."

"I don't want to see you, or hear about you for the rest of my life. Do you understand, you little meddlesome weasel?"

"Yes."

"For Steph's sake, I might not file the charge, might. Now, get out of here and never come back!"

Martin thought he'd pass out, but he managed to back out and drove away. "Why did I do this?" he wailed.

Hughes shook her head and walked back across Seigniory Avenue. She'd made a video recording on her phone and would check it when she was back at her apartment.

Martin's jaw tightened. He blubbered as he drove, "Hughes could be a cold-blooded killer! And no one, not even the police, seem to care. She's clever alright. She had me cornered. The question is how did she know that I'd be back. She told me she'd expected something, but why?" Martin never thought of himself as a loose cannon, he remained oblivious. That small, single tirade had Martin feeling better about himself already, until he looked over and saw the dirty paper towels. Unlike himself, grinding his teeth, he began to speed.

CHAPTER FIFTY-TWO

CONNOR RUSHED AROUND the condo with a towel around his waist, seeing that everything was in place. He had farm-fresh eggs for a spinach omelet. His sliced potatoes with thinly shaved garlic were ready for frying up, and the French bread was ready for toasting. The California Chardonnay was chilling, and the lights were dimmed just right. Connor checked himself in the hall mirror and was surprised to see bags under his eyes, and hollow cheeks. Stressed, but excited to see Timothy, he fidgeted while he waited. *Will the bloody case ever end?*

Timothy called to say he'd arrived in downtown Montreal and would be at the condo in fifteen minutes. Connor went down to the entrance to meet him. He checked his clothes, a navy cotton sweater, a rounded neck with the slightest hint of a collar, narrow gray pants and shoes without socks. He wore a silver Rolex and a gold signet ring. Beauty and simplicity, with a fatigue and a nervousness that he didn't fully understand. Was he in love? He'd never been able to love a man, feel weak in the knees and be vulnerable. That was the trade of tabloid rags.

Timothy approached the entrance carrying two suitcases, his mass of curls blowing in the wind, and with a smile that struck Connor's heart. A knowing look passed between them, passionate and urgent. Timothy dropped his bags and they embraced. Not a word passed between them. Then Timothy whispered hoarsely, "We'd better go up." Connor grabbed one bag and led the way. Inside the apartment, Connor said, "I have everything ready for a light dinner."

"It can wait." Timothy put his hand around the back of Connor's head and pulled him so close that they felt each other's breaths on their necks. Clothes fell like rain, and they lay together on the sheets. Their hands traced the flesh of their backs and buttocks and legs until they could no longer hold off. Finally satiated, they lay entwined, glistening in the dark. They fell asleep and forgot about food.

In the very early hours, Connor shook and cried out, "Don't, don't." He began to shake angrily in his sleep. His arm swung out, catching Timothy's back. "Connor, Connor! Wake up! It's okay. I'm here."

"What?"

"You were having a nightmare."

"Did I say anything?"

"I was asleep. You woke me, but I couldn't make anything out."

"You sure?"

"Yes. I'll get the sheet. It's on the floor somewhere. We can both get some sleep. I'm here with you, Connor. Try to sleep. It's not even four yet."

Connor tried. The warmth of Timothy's body helped him, and he finally fell asleep. An hour later, he awoke and envied Timothy who slept on. It was comforting to watch him. Moments later, he felt abandoned again. *Why did the case have to be reopened? Why did Devon have to die?* He had to get up and pull himself together.

Connor rose at five-thirty and was in the kitchen converting the light dinner into breakfast. Bleary-eyed, Timothy stumbled into the kitchen. "We could have waited, but I am famished. Connor, no one makes an omelet or these potatoes like you. We don't have bread like this in Florida, and I have looked, I can assure you. Never mind toasting it."

"There's more if you want it." Haltingly, Connor looked straight at Timothy, and said, "I missed you."

"Same here."

"When I saw you arriving with your bags, looking hopeful, I felt love for the first time. I never knew what it was or how it felt."

"I loved you, Connor, even when you unceremoniously booted me out of the relationship and the condo. The quality of mercy and all that."

"I don't need your mercy."

"Connor, I'm kidding. I meant I love you whatever comes."

"I didn't understand. Sorry."

"What in particular has you so on edge? You can trust me; you should know that."

"The detectives reworking my parents' case are the best apparently. They have me in their sights for murder. I know it. Em has some incriminating evidence that would help them charge me."

"Tell me exactly what she has, and how she came by it."

Connor related what Emma had written.

"Look, Connor, you know my mother died from breast cancer. What suffering! It was a horrific family journey. She was the heart of our family. But, Connor, the day she died, I felt someone had punched me in the gut. I couldn't breathe. Tears just flowed. But that very day, in the back of my head, I felt relief. I was selfish. What you felt was normal for the troubled relationship you had with your father. The seconds seem longer when someone dies. Ideas can be exaggerated. Why can't Emma see that? She's your older sister, her brother's keeper if we want to get biblical."

"These cops are good at working her, her moral sensibility. Duty to our parents who are vulnerable and can't defend themselves. She must help them put things right. Em was actually about to give me the agenda, but I made the mistake of telling her I was looking for it, and she pulled back. Underneath her morality, Em is afraid I killed them both."

"But the police tested you, took your clothes and questioned you and searched the house."

"I know. I remind her of that. We have to get that book. Can I really trust you, Timothy?"

"You can."

"I realized when Em was in the hospital that all three sets of detectives have made one error."

"Which is?"

"That night, I gagged and vomited following three hours of questioning. I had been forced to stay in the same room with my parents. I cried out, 'I can't sleep here!' I called you and you said I could bunk in with you. The cops probably thought I meant some friend on the street, but I drove downtown."

"So?"

"They forgot to search my car."

"Shit!"

"You can never reveal that to anyone. I'm done if you do, Timothy. I will be convicted on probable cause."

"You have my word."

"I have to pray they don't discover their error. That's why Em can't help them arrest me. They'd put the gun and change of clothes in the car they never searched."

"We'll get the book." Timothy's love was human. *Was the gun in the car, and if that, what else?* Doubt began to chip away at Timothy. Again.

CHAPTER FIFTY-THREE

DETECTIVES DAMIANO AND Matte felt their soft approach with Emma Tibbett had moved them an inch closer to her finally revealing what additional information she had not disclosed. "If we could only discover if Connor Tibbett knew about his father's intention to strike him from any inheritance in favor of his sister, we'd have some new information to use when we bring him in for questioning," Damiano said. "Otherwise, we're just as flummoxed as the detectives that preceded us," she added dejectedly.

"We're going to read through the case point by point. Somebody missed something, and we are missing it too."

The phone rang. "Damn! Damn again. It's Zagan *again*! He'll be the death of me. Detective Damiano."

"Doctor Zagan."

"I know."

"I see, well, I have the results of your latest scan, and the results are unchanged."

I'll finally be rid of him. "Truthfully, I'm not surprised, Doctor. That's it then. I can breathe again."

"I remain unconvinced. I still feel this could be a very early carcinoma. I would like you to make an appointment with a thoracic surgeon, Doctor Solange. I've sent him your scans. His number is…"

"Doctor, this affair has me very stressed and I…"

"Detective, I am being cautious for your life. Please, understand that."

"Well, this caution is killing me!"

"I'm happy that you have a sense of humor."

"I don't."

"Call Solange, please. It's the last request I'll make, I hope."

"I will. Thank you."

"You're welcome, young lady."

Damiano hung up. "He even got that wrong."

"If he's in his sixties, forty is young." The doctor had been on speaker phone. "Just do what he asks. Then, you'll be secure and finished with him."

Damiano was about to add… then the phone rang. "We need some peace. Leave the call on speaker again. Would you take it Pierre?"

"Detective Matte."

"Brian Barrett, Detective. I'm still aware you said you'd be calling me again. When I had the time, I did some research that has had good results for me. The night of the murders, I told you I was working fourteen-hour days as a result of losing the house, at least one hundred thousand dollars of it. At the time, I was overworked, still numb with grief, so I rarely paid attention to non-essentials, other than work. There was a man who'd open the front door of the building after hours. Even when I saw him recently, my memory of the man was foggy.

"I was hoping they might have video footage saved in their archives, but no such luck. Turns out though, this Mr. Tigh kept a log and wrote in our names. I had no recollection of that. He's seventy-one, still at the desk and keeps old logs at home. He brought the log I needed to work, and I asked him to sign an affidavit to ascertain that I was at work that night. I even offered him money which he refused. Do you want me to bring in the log and affidavit or send them to you?"

Matte saw that Damiano was about to pound the desk, so he raised a warning arm. "You can send them by express post."

"I'll use UPS."

"Good work."

"Thank you. By the way, you won't need to question my wife for whom I was paying a therapist to help with her grief and guilt. I've learned she was taking full advantage of his comfort. She has lived with the fact that I can't forgive her. That might have been the reason she sought forgiveness elsewhere. I was even forced to have a paternity test to discover if Piper was my daughter. Thank the stars, she is. We had plans to separate. Piper only recognizes photos of Calvin. Perhaps, the only place where I'm decisive is my clinic. I hated my wife, but I do love her and the son we shared. If we separated, Calvin's memory would diminish and fade with time. We love each other and we want to keep the family we started in its totality, tears and loss included. We are also victims of the horror of that Thursday. But we survived."

"Detective Damiano and I meet people in the throes of great turmoil and sadness. Sometimes, we meet good people with our values. You are a strong man, Doctor, and we both wish you a good life."

"I appreciate that. I want you both to find the person who made victims of so many."

"We are dedicated to that end."

CHAPTER FIFTY-FOUR

DETECTIVES DAMIANO AND Matte studied each page of both reports until five. "We have to close this case soon. The chief gave us two weeks. I'm bringing the rest home with me. Jeff is at some dinner I backed out of, and Luke is in a chess tournament at McGill. I'll also have the bloody doctor's call. Don't remind me I'm receiving excellent care or I'll throw my pen at you."

"Who taught Luke chess?"

"Who do you think? Do you play, Pierre?"

"I quite enjoy it."

"Are you some master?"

"Not far from, I guess."

"Luke would love a game. You have to come to dinner."

"Happily."

"Why is everything about you so proper, even your language. What's wrong with 'sure' instead of 'happily'? This threat of lung cancer is beginning to hit me again. Forget what I said."

"Don't let it – you're as healthy as a horse."

"Why a thoracic surgeon?"

"You'll find out tonight. No more Ativan."

"I saved two, so I don't need your help."

"I'm home tonight for a call."

"You're a real pal."

"I know."

When Damiano walked into the house, an uncomfortable silence engulfed her. Taking out her phone, she placed it in the middle of the kitchen table and unloaded the old case files there as well. By seven o'clock the specialist hadn't called, and she was on her fourth glass of wine without food. Checking her phone, it almost slipped out of her hand. "If he doesn't call soon, I'm not going to answer!"

She opened the freezer and took Luke's frozen pizza, placed it into the oven and forgot about it. The edges of the pizza curled and blackened. "Dammit!" She grabbed oven mitts and slid the pizza onto a dinner plate and poured herself half a glass of wine. She took three bites. "There isn't one thing on this carboard that tastes remotely like a pizza. This isn't cheese, the pepperoni is fake and the dough is like pressed wood. Ugh!" Out went the remains of the pizza.

She began to read everything on Connor Tibbett the night of the murders. "Forensics took his clothes, examined every part of him, especially his hair. Any cartridge residue, GSR, would have certainly lodged itself there. For the next five days, he was examined, without results." She read the detailed search of the house. Even the drains had been searched. "Like us, they were confounded by the absence of a weapon." Damiano put down the file sheet and tried to think. Instead, her head first slumped on her hand, then on the table.

When her phone rang, its sound struck her like a bullet. "Jeff?"

"Doctor Solange."

No doctor would call at nine forty-one unless the matter was serious. Damiano struggled to appear calm. "Yes, Doctor."

"Ms. Toni Damiano?"

"Yes."

"Sorry for the late call, you're my first call. I'm just out of surgery."

Oh, God!

"Don't be nervous. I see nothing to be nervous about. I have all three of your scans. And, I see nothing."

Damiano was certain he could hear her sigh of relief.

"I'd like you to come down to the General for a test that takes about five hours. Simply, we're checking your lungs and breathing. I'll check in with you during the test."

"Is this like a stress test? I'm mixed up. You're a thoracic surgeon, and I'm not trying to be difficult, but what's the connection?"

"Doctor Zagan is a personal friend. Yes, like a stress test. You can book it with my secretary any time you want. There is no rush."

"This is finally good news."

"From me, yes. Doctor Zagan is a thorough man."

"Who came close to costing me my sanity."

Doctor Solange had a warm laugh. "Book the appointment on your time frame, and goodnight."

Damiano took the news on board and jumped shouting, "Thank you, God, thank you!"

Emma Tibbett regretted inviting Phillip Shore to visit the family at seven-thirty that evening. With her meds reduced, her leg began to throb and a searing headache was already peaking. Mrs. Dianne Dupont, from the CLSC, had just left for the day. Emma barely had time to appreciate her agony before her boys burst through the front door like wild mustangs. They were Emma's little boys again. They flung their arms around Emma's neck, charging both cheeks with kisses, sloppy kisses that smelled of boys. Emma loved it.

"Devon's father wants to meet us. I said he would be welcome after dinner. What do we do for dinner?"

"Not to worry Mom, I'm making beans and my special hotdogs, enough for everyone. Best of all, we wash dishes now. Don't even think of moving. I'll make you salmon sandwiches, no coffee, milk."

"Yes, sir," Emma said smiling.

In no time, they were all in the living room, the boys sitting cross-legged around Emma. The beans and dogs were demolished, their questions, continuous and their smiles, loving. "Okay, guys, we wash the dishes, brush our teeth, quick wash and get back down to meet Dad's father."

Emma was still eating. "I hardly recognize you guys, what happened?"

"Dad taught us to clean up. He ordered us to grow up, and we did," Terry answered smugly.

"This isn't a dream, is it?"

"Nope, we're real," Bobby laughed.

When Emma had eaten as much as she could, Michael took her plate. Minutes later he appeared with a toothbrush, loaded with Colgate, and a pot filled half way with water. "Here, you can brush too. Here's a wet facecloth. You look great, just like you are."

"May I ask one favor?"

"Anything."

"I am very tired and sore. How about we all visit here for half an hour, and then you boys can visit downstairs. The deadline is nine."

"I'll take care of that, Mom. You look good, I mean it."

Emma forced a smile.

The boys were ready when the bell rang. The man they met at the door was an older version of their father. Six-foot, or near, salt and pepper hair, a ready smile saddened by events, and a warm hand.

"Come in, Phillip," Emma said kindly. "Meet your grandsons, Michael, Bobby and Terry." The boys shook hands, a little awkwardly, but willingly.

"Hello!" Shyness prevented the boys from saying more.

Phillip Shore walked over to Emma on the hospital bed that had been set up in the living room. He bent over and gently hugged her. "Thank you so much for this. I feel awfully alone. You've done a fine job with the boys. And I know you did all the work alone."

"Dad came back." Michael tried not to raise his voice. "He taught us to take responsibility. Would you like to see our rooms? They're tidy."

"You should have seen the mess before," Terry said, jumping in. The talking began and it didn't stop. Emma listened and quietly wept. *He did want to come back!*

Half an hour later, Michael noticed his mother was fading, and led Shore and his brothers downstairs. "Perhaps I should go."

"No, Mom said we could talk down here till nine." Shore's face softened as he listened. "You're my grandsons. Maybe I can arrange for you to visit us in Toronto. I'll cover the trip. Your grandmother hasn't seen you since you were infants."

At eight-thirty, Michael sent his two younger brothers up to prepare for bed. They left reluctantly. Michael told Shore about his pursuit of the boy who had threatened his mother's life. "I had to do something. My mom could have died." He told his story excitedly and in one breath. "I thought of Mom having to face the police, so I ran back with my bad knee and..." Michael gulped more air and continued. "I told Dad the whole story and he listened. He said I acted like a man, not a boy. I was proud. I wish my dad was still here."

Shore said quietly, "You've given me a real gift, Michael. I won't ever forget."

After Michael saw Phillip Shore out the side door, he returned to the living room. His heart fell when he saw that his mother was fast asleep with her clothes on. He had forgotten to help her change before Shore arrived. He swore that that would never happen again. Her left foot was sticking out of the blanket. The rest of the blanket was bunched across her chest and under her chin. Michael saw how small his mother looked and fragile. He felt a chill. She'd needed his help to change, but he was too busy in his desire to tell his story to his grandfather. He would never again forget that his mother had never abandoned them, like his father. She alone had washed him and his brothers, fed them, comforted them, taught each of them to ride a bike, and loved them and worked to support them. That night he had failed her. Before the accident, he was a teenager, a kid, and now, Michael saw that his youth was lost in the collateral damage of the accident. He thought like a man – he was a man. He covered his mother with a second blanket.

A little after three that morning, Emma woke in a panic. She needed the bathroom and, though a walker was next to the sofa, her fear of falling immobilized her. She reached for her phone and called Michael. "Son, I need you."

Michael took a few seconds to shake off the sleep before he awkwardly jumped into his jeans, almost toppling to the floor. He was awake then. Nothing would rouse his brothers. He guessed the problem when he found his mother sitting on the sofa.

"Bathroom, right?" he whispered. "Lean on me, Mom. Forget the crutches. I'll wait outside."

When Emma was safely tucked in again, she had her old smile back. "I won't forget this, son."

"You changed my diapers, Mom. It's the least I can do to help you. Go back to sleep."

"Mrs. Dupont from the CLSC will set me up tomorrow. Don't worry. I'm home and that's what counts."

Michael smiled. He liked being needed.

CHAPTER FIFTY-FIVE

THAT SAME NIGHT, pacing around her apartment, Sandra wondered what she should do about Martin Heron. While she thought him ridiculous, she also considered him potentially dangerous. So unnerved, she'd lost a whole day of her artwork, a quiet pastel view of the St-Anne-de Bellevue boardwalk, deserted in April. Since James's death, she valued time. A day lost was part of life lost. She considered filing a stalking charge, or a restraining order, but read they rarely worked. She also thought of contacting the detectives investigating the Tibbett case. *Bloody hell!* She abandoned the last option because she'd appear as ridiculous as Heron.

Before he died, James had told her not to burn bridges. She'd been reading Edith Piaf's biography. Piaf's purported last words were: "Every damn thing you do in this life you pay for." Faulkner had said the past was never past. Hughes could feel its breath on her neck. James was her husband. His tragedy and all that went with it had brought her into its swirl and aftermath. Hughes had survived her own surgery, a weighty survivor's guilt and a grief that never left her. There was no freedom; there never would be. She saw that now.

Heron had built his own Frankenstein from guilt, supposition, and a need to be avenged or just noticed. His creation needed her injured to keep it alive. That was the reason he was dangerous; the reason she was forced to act. She was on edge when she made her call. She could almost see Heron cringing, backing away from the call. He answered before it went to voicemail. "Martin, this is Sandra Hughes. I'm hoping we can talk this out without seeking legal action."

Heron said nothing.

"I know you are thinking of Steph, maybe, the time lost between you, maybe grief. Grief is a lifetime partner. No amount of anger can rid you of grief, I know from experience. You wish you could change your story with Steph, but sadly you can't. We'd all like to have a second chance with loved ones we've lost. For the time being, I'm holding on to the video of you stalking me."

"I think someone is out to get me." His voice was suddenly shrill. "I could have been killed!"

Sandra knew she had to play this right. "My God, what happened?" The kindness in her voice compelled Martin to recount the Ogilvy's department episode. "They thought that I had fainted on the escalator, or had a panic attack. I was sure I was pushed. I could tell they thought I was some nutcase."

Sandra continued her soothing tone. "I hope you went to the hospital to have yourself checked out. Escalators have caused terrible injuries."

"No, I didn't. I heard someone utter the word paranoia behind me and I walked out. I even thought that you might be behind the attack."

"Martin, you're scaring me. I was nowhere near Ogilvy's."

"I know what I know."

"Are you actually accusing me?"

Martin didn't answer.

"Don't force me to act. Your anger and yes, paranoia, frighten me. I am assuming you don't want the new *1510 West* community newspaper, very popular with West Islanders, getting a hold of this Ogilvy's story and the stalking video."

"You wouldn't dare!"

"Think of the headline: Respected Montreal Citizen Dumpster Diving!"

Heron's voice shook with dread. "I can't have this. Why, it would destroy me, destroy me!"

"I don't want to do that."

"You're a bitch, a real bitch." Martin fought back like a kid already on the ground with the bully ready to punch him in the face.

"I am not, Martin. I'm a woman whose life was gutted as I watched my husband battle until he died. We lived that horror for almost two years. I know pain, humiliation and grief. I won't stand aside for more of it. Do you hear me, Martin? I mean every word I say."

Again, silence while Heron tried to regain composure.

"What are you going to do with the video?"

"That depends on you, Martin. I'll repeat what I said to you. Steph was my friend. I would never implicate her in anything illegal, let alone a murder. When my husband died, I just wanted to grieve and live my life. I never wanted to forget James. I had been ill and I wanted to live because I was afraid of dying. I'd seen how quickly life is lost, what small space we occupy in this world. Life passes in a day. The universal lament, there just wasn't enough time, rings daily in my ears."

Silence.

"Are you still there, Martin? Are you hearing me?"

"I think I've made a real blunder."

"Nothing that can't be fixed?"

"You won't hear from me again."

"I'll delete the video."

Martin still wasn't convinced, but he recognized a gut punch.

Sandra hung up and put the video in a safe place. She wasn't taking any chances.

CHAPTER FIFTY-SIX

IT HAD BEEN A SECOND tumultuous night for Connor and Timothy. Again, Connor had nightmares and struck out in his sleep. "You can't, you can't!" This cry was followed by a dangerous swipe that caught Timothy across the neck. He sat up gasping. Coughing, Timothy grabbed a blanket and pillow, then changed his mind. He shook Connor gently to wake him up.

"What the blazes is it?" Connor groaned.

"I know you're half asleep, but you cried out again and struck me on the neck. These night terrors you're having could really injure me. You have to see someone about it. No wonder you are so tired, and I don't feel safe with you at night. You're smart, Connor. It's explosive anxiety, and we both know the reasons. It began with this investigation. I was awake a good part of the night, and I began to think of Rodion Raskolnikov and his suffering and, finally, his need to confess. We studied *Crime and Punishment*, remember? He thought himself an extraordinary fellow who could overcome his guilt, but he failed."

Connor sat up and was about to put an end to the talk, but changed his mind.

"Why did you tell me about your car not being searched? What do I do with that, except think you hid that gun there or worse? Why tell me at all? You know Emma. Why have an outburst you know will frighten her? You also knew she'd write down the whole tirade in that book of hers. Like Raskolnikov, you want your secrets out. What is all this self-torture getting you? Do you want to turn yourself in to the police? You have to meet with Emma. I'm sure she has no idea that the damn book, or its threat, is killing you. Clear that threat up first. Then, we can deal with the rest. I'll go with you if you want."

Connor changed the conversation. "My father won't let go of me, even though he's dead. The cops are on my back. Three investigations, three! Why don't they close the case and leave me be? I was sixteen when my father said, 'You're a real pretty boy, with little substance.' That was his summation of me. I'm handsome, but empty. I had never said anything to provoke him. I avoided him. He walked into my room, blew past the "Knock" sign on the door and said those words. I was trying to remember just one time he actually held me. He must have before I was five, but never after that age. He never even spanked me. I was ignored."

"Your father's dead. He's not after anyone. He has no power except the power you give him. You have to let go, Connor."

Connor took another abrupt turn in the conversation. "You never asked me what was in the car?"

"I figure you'll tell me on your own."

Connor stood staring down at Timothy. "You've never asked me if I killed my parents."

Timothy stalled. "I came back, didn't I?"

Connor's jaw tightened. "It's important that I know what you think. It's important for us to go on, to be together. I need a straight answer."

"Look, Connor, I assume that Emma suggested in that agenda of hers, that you might have murdered your parents. She has troubling doubts. I love you with everything that love entails. I know you wanted something from your father you never received. All the necessary elements: love, recognition and acceptance."

"Can't you give me a straight answer?"

"Alright, no, I hope not, but Connor I'm not sure. Why don't you tell me, and I'll believe you?"

"I hoped you wouldn't need to ask the question."

"Why are you so frightened of what Emma will say?"

"The cops need closure, and I'm their boy. What better proof than a sister accusing her brother."

"Did you take the gun? The car was a perfect place to hide it and dispose of it."

"Why can't anyone leave me alone? I'd like your support, not your freakin' questions. Do you understand?"

"Do you want to see Emma alone then?"

"No, she trusts you."

"Good. We'll go together. Call her. I have to go into the office at one, so tonight is best."

Emma slept soundly like her boys and woke when she heard them in the bathroom. In minutes, they roared down the stairs and kissed her. Terry shouted back on his way to the kitchen, "Shower every second day, sponge wash today. Toast, Mom?"

"Oh, yes. Any chance of coffee?"

"Instant."

"Fine." Emma loved to hear their noises again. There were days she thought she might not make it. She'd heard the doctors.

"Toast and plum jelly and black coffee," Michael said. "We'll clean up after we eat. Whatever you do, don't put any weight on your bad leg. The walker helps you up, the crutches are for getting around. The CLSC lady will help you to change those clothes. We didn't want to wake you once you fell asleep."

"I'm glad you didn't. Best sleep I've had in days."

"We will stay at school for lunch, so you two can work things out alone."

"What about money?"

"Connor has given me some."

"He gave me money as well. See you after school."

Perhaps it was because of her condition, but she was amazed at the speed of her boys. One second, they were kissing her, the next, they were out the door. At nine, Mrs. Dupont was at the front door, reading a small note. "The door is open."

"Good morning, Dianne."

"I see you are in good spirits. First things first: bathroom and a sponge bath, change clothes, breakfast, then, rehab."

"I'm tired already," Emma joked.

Dianne was in her fifties, married with children, a practical woman who Emma took to immediately. She had a busy life, Kyle, an autistic eleven-year-old, and fifteen-year-old Julie. "My philosophy is don't waste time on yesterday, or tomorrow will catch you off guard. Now, let's sponge you down."

Dianne worked so quickly and thoroughly that Emma had no time to be shy. "What do you have in clothes that won't have to be cut to get on over the plaster?"

"I have a new pair of sweat pants that I was going to return because they were too large."

"Perfect. Where do I find them?"

"Main dresser, second drawer."

When Emma was dressed in sweats and a long-sleeved cotton top, she was ready for rehab.

"Rule number one: don't ever put yourself in a position where you could fall. A fall can ruin a summer or take a life. I've seen both. Put your right hand on the side of the bed, your left on the walker. I'm here to prevent a fall. Now, pull yourself up.

"Good! Here are your crutches. No weight on that bad leg. Can you manage a few steps? You've cheated. You've had experience."

"I've had boys."

"Even better. Let's walk together. I'm right beside you. You're a natural."

"Alright! I have a favor to ask you. I want to make or have the boys make pasta for dinner, but I haven't any sauce left. It's a simple recipe. We have no tomatoes but the canned ones will do. Beside the stove, I keep my recipe books in a silver box. It should be the third one down. I'll find the page for you."

"No problem." Dianne found the box easily, scooped up the third book and opened it. She began to read and stopped abruptly. She made her way back to the living room. "I don't think this is a recipe book."

Emma took the agenda. "No, it's not." Emma saw the lock was gone. Her stress was back. Dianne made the sauce, but Emma was emotionally absent. The last page was missing too. At least, she thought she remembered a last page.

CHAPTER FIFTY-SEVEN

EMMA HAD TWO HOURS to herself before the boys came home from school. She fingered the agenda. Who broke the lock? Reading the last few pages troubled her. Wasn't there another page? She seemed to recall writing it, but she couldn't be certain. Dissociative amnesia the doctor called it. It often occurred after a traumatic event. Her heart skipped when the phone rang, and she hesitated when she saw that the caller was Connor.

"Hi, Em. Timothy and I would like to drop by after dinner for a short visit. I'll have hamburger meat, buns, milk and condiments for tomorrow. The boys will devour all of it in no time. About seven? One hour, tops."

Emma couldn't refuse, and Connor knew that, not after all the help he'd given her. "Phillip Shore, Devon's father met the boys last night." The interjection eased the tension. "I fell asleep, and they talked downstairs. The visit was good for the boys and Phillip. An aging copy of Devon."

"Still, difficult for you though."

"Somewhat soothing but painful. See you both tonight then."

"One hour, Em. No more."

For the next two hours, her leg throbbed and she felt a migraine coming on.

Detectives Damiano and Matte were scouring the files looking for the 'miss,' "It's something to do with Tibbett. They searched him, allowed him to sleep at a friend's house after he threw up and had been put through three hours of interrogation. They called this Timothy Lang who verified that Tibbett was going to his place. A friend nearby? Holy Shit!"

"They never verified where this kid lived," Matte added, not without some excitement.

"What if he had to use his car?" Damiano said like a cat with a mouse in its paws.

"That's it!"

Damiano could barely contain herself. "There is no evidence that either team searched the car, ever."

"That's where the gun was hidden. We go to the chief with this and the suggested change of inheritance. Maybe this Timothy Lang, wasn't a next-door neighbor, but a frat brother who lived in the McGill ghetto. Tibbett just drove away from the crime scene, and no one stopped him."

"When we interrogate Tibbett, we pretend that we already know he drove to his friend's house. We can't allow him to work out that we've caught onto the car. Thing is, the detectives never thought to search the car at all. They all assumed Tibbett hadn't left the house once he found his parents. By the time they might have thought of the car, it had been driven off the premises."

"Before we meet with the chief, we set our pegs in order: Tibbett found the bodies, had the opportunity to murder his parents, had motive, rejection and abandonment by the father, and a deep-seated animosity. We have the added knowledge of the disinheritance. Lastly, we now know where the weapon was hidden. Suicide-murder, or a double murder, the jury is still out. But obstruction of justice is in. We also have some degree of hope we can break Tibbett down."

Inside Chief Donat's office, Damiano summarized their findings. Donat sat behind his desk on his elevated custom chair that gave him the additional height he wished he actually had. In his brown suit, crisp white shirt and a knit brown tie, he was a very tidy man. Donat still wore a watch, larger than his wrist, that he used to time interviews. He steeled his blue eyes on Damiano and listened attentively. He rarely asked you to repeat. "I was hoping for more. Circumstantial evidence is what we have. That and wishful hope that you can break Tibbett down. Bring him in. Prepare tough questions for the interrogation room. Tibbett has had years to figure out the questions and the answers, but he won't be prepared for the fact that we know he drove his car from the scene. Go hard on this new evidence. Don't give him a chance to come up with a plausible reply. Now get him in here!"

"It wasn't a howling endorsement." Damiano sighed, walking back to the murder room. "Donat knows that the catastrophic blunder with the car can blow up our whole case. What do you gather from the chief?"

"What I expected. We go with what we have. Our allotted time for this case is almost up."

They walked back slowly to the murder room where Damiano prepared to make the call. They had to be careful. This was their last go with Tibbett. They needed reliable answers to their questions. But Damiano was also aware that after ten and a half years later, memory is not precise. There would be distortions when Tibbett tried to recall his actual movements that night keeping in mind that he was highly stressed. Stress can interfere with memory. The brain surrenders to primal fear and self-preservation.

Damiano made the call.

When Tibbett answered, Damiano already detected a fear Tibbett was trying to conceal. "Again?"

"Yes, at nine tomorrow morning at the Crémazie Division. You'll be met at the door, of course."

"I have work. Can't we rearrange this to a later time?"

"We'll see you at nine, Mr. Tibbett."

Connor crushed the phone in his hand and it left bruises on his palm. "Shit! Em has to back me. Or, fuck! I'm done."

CHAPTER FIFTY-EIGHT

EMMA TRIED TO MAINTAIN a happy face with the boys. She ate too much pasta and felt bloated. The boys were simultaneously boisterous and sad. "Mom, Dad's father looks like Dad, just older. I wish he was still alive," Terry spoke for his brothers. "I think Dad really cared for us."

"Why wouldn't he?" Emma said tenderly.

Michael took over. "We are still lucky to have you, Mom. You never left us and we know how often we were little pigs."

"There were times I was tempted."

The boys' heads flew back.

"Can't a mother kid?"

They sighed loudly. "I knew you were kidding," Bobby said.

"Mrs. Dupont found my agenda in my recipe basket in the kitchen. Does anyone know how it got there?"

"I do. I do." Terry jumped up from the table "Dad took it. He said he would hide it and give it to you when you got home. I thought he'd hide it at his place, but I guess he hid it here instead. And, Uncle Connor offered me fifty dollars to find it so he could read it. I said you might have thrown it out. He tried to pretend the agenda didn't really matter. Why offer me fifty bucks if it didn't matter? He was lying!" Terry was gleeful.

"The nurses told me that Connor never left my room for two days when I was semi-comatose." Emma felt she had to defend her brother.

"Yeah, Uncle Connor brought food too. He's not so bad, but he's not our dad," Bobby said with conviction.

"At seven Uncle Connor and Timothy..."

"I thought he was history," Michael said knowingly.

"They are trying again to work things out. I'm glad."

"That's what Dad was trying to do, right Mom?" Bobby said.

"Yes, son. Uncle Connor and Timothy are bringing all the fixings for burgers for tomorrow."

"That's okay by me," Terry said, looking more interested.

"After we all say hello, I need to talk to them about my care and other things. You'd be a great help if you did your homework downstairs."

"I know what you're going to discuss. It's the ..."

"Alright, Michael, that's enough."

"Mom is back!" he kidded.

"Most of me anyway."

The boys caught the serious tone and quieted down. Emma felt a pang of guilt because her boys had been so supportive. "They're only staying for an hour, and the house is yours again."

When the doorbell rang, a nervous shiver shot through most of them. Emma ran a hand through her hair, the boys stood by the front door. The living room was on the right, so Emma was aware of their arrival. Michael opened the door. Timothy walked in behind Connor, stepped forward and greeted them all warmly. "You guys have grown like weeds. Good to see you again," Timothy said, extending his hand.

The boys were quick to respond.

"Mom, can we play games after our homework?"

"Certainly."

Timothy and Connor sat in separate chairs close to Emma. "I'm not ganging up on you, Em. The detectives have called me in for an interrogation tomorrow at nine. They must have found new evidence. They know of your near-death accident, so they will leave you alone. I..." Connor was visibly shaken.

Emma hadn't noticed his hollowed cheeks and weight loss because her attention had been on herself. Compared to Timothy, who had that hint of a Florida tan and a mass of sandy hair, Connor looked ill.

Why Emma brought up the agenda, she didn't know, and would take some time to forgive herself.

Connor blurted out, "Terry told you about the fifty dollars. I only wanted to see what I had said. That's all. I would never have taken it."

Timothy took over. "Your brother can't sleep. He cries out at night, all because of an outburst of his wounded soul. Those wounds were caused by your father. When Devon left you alone with three young kids, I'm sure you're human, Emma, and said a few things about kids you didn't mean. Imagine if Connor had written those thoughts down and now threatened to let the boys read them. I am not trying to hurt you, Emma, I'm trying to help your brother."

Connor rubbed his eyes. "All I'm asking you, sis, is to let the detectives do their own work. Apparently, they have, or I wouldn't have been summoned. You're my sister. Don't help them nail me."

Emma wept. The boys had snuck up the stairs and knelt just behind the door, ready to barge in and defend their mother. They had listened to every word. The boys were breathing hard. Michael held them back.

"Connor, Timothy is right. You're both right. I am deeply sorry for all the sleepless nights. The agenda was childish. I'll dispose of it. I felt I had some moral compass that no one has. I'm positive I said some brutal epithets about kids that I never meant. I love you, Connor. My thoughts will be with you tomorrow. What a tragedy for our family, and you've carried the brunt of it because you found Mom and Dad."

"Thank you, Em. It's a night terror, and has been for ten and a half years. Maybe, finally, the end will come." Connor rose and went to hug his sister. "How did all this happen to our family? We're just ordinary people leading mundane lives."

Emma blubbered. "You know the answer, Con. Why not us?"

"I suppose," Connor sighed.

The boys crept back downstairs. Connor and Timothy left.

"Call me, Connor."

"I will."

CHAPTER FIFTY-NINE

Driving back home to Grand Boulevard in Notre-Dame-de-Grace, Timothy invited Connor to their twice-a-year restaurant, Le Club Chasse et Pêche near Old Montreal on rue St-Claude. Connor looked at his wrist, tight on the wheel, and thought if he were to bend it, he'd be looking at a fracture. He was that stiff. "I won't sleep tonight, so I need something light. A toasted tomato sandwich and a green salad. I don't want The Last Supper. We both know how that went."

"Fine with me."

"And, Timothy, I'll sleep on my sofa."

"I don't mind the sofa. I can sleep anywhere."

"I want you to have the bed."

After they ate, Connor said, "I'm using my last week of vacation for the mess I'm in, so I'll still receive my usual cheque. I used my first week for Emma's hospitalization. You may have to bail me out. I'll reimburse you, of course."

Timothy sat quietly surrounded by wet tension.

"Thank you for coming back to this load of rot. I need to organize my thoughts tonight. You've brought books, I hope."

"I'm fine. If you need to talk, all you have to do is call me."

"I know that."

The night was too long. Connor pounded his pillow, fought with the blanket, rubbed his stinging eyes, tried to rearrange tangling thoughts and aching limbs. Morning came too soon. Connor had showered, grabbed something to eat, and was ready to leave by seven.

"Call me if you need me, or just to tell me you're there. I presume you'll be early."

"Time to think."

Timothy nodded.

Connor's tension had moved him beyond the possibility of any cogent conversation. They parted with a hug. Connor drove east along

Sherbrooke Street, turned north onto rue St-Denis, and eventually turned onto the Crémazie service road that took him west under the Metropolitan Expressway until he recognized the cold, gray Division building. He parked in the visitors' parking in the front, smiling ruefully at the word *visitors*. Before he left, Timothy had said, "You look good." He wasn't up to their usual reply. "I have to, I'm gay."

He was almost forty-five minutes early. He wondered if truth really was a release, or another lie. He recalled having sessions with a therapist a few times, after his parents' death. He had told Connor, "Tell me about your feelings for your father, you'll experience an unburdening." He hadn't. He'd given the therapist a thread of himself, and like a knitted wool sweater, he felt his life unravelling. Naked is what he felt, and weaker. He drank water from the plastic bottle he always kept in the car. For a few minutes, his head relaxed against the seat and he dozed off. At once he was pinioned by the weight of his demons and he jerked awkwardly striking the wheel. "Shit!" It was slushy outside and not conducive to walking around, so he sat locked in his car for the next forty minutes gnawing his nails.

Detective Matte was opening the door as he approached. Detective Damiano was standing next to him. Matte and Damiano saw the dark blazer, collarless white shirt, tan pants, Italian shoes with no socks. Connor also wore a loosely-tied navy cashmere scarf. Matte greeted him, Connor nodded, and followed them without a word. Matte left them when they reached the interview room on the sixth floor. Connor hated small spaces and balked when he saw the size of the room. Damiano gestured for him to sit across from her. Connor tried to calm himself by crossing his long legs, but only succeeded in striking the camera under the small diamond-shaped table. He looked up nervously and noticed the other cameras in the corners of the room. Every breath he took would be studied like a bug under a microscope. He also suspected Detective Matte was in another room monitoring the questioning. Damiano pretended not to notice Connor's nervousness and opened the thick dossier in front of her.

Damiano looked up at Connor. "Let's begin with you arriving home that Thursday night." Before Connor spoke, Damiano opened the formal interview stating her name. rank, date and time. She asked him to introduce himself. Following the formal opening, Damiano read Connor his rights.

Suspect! That was clear now. Connor's shirt was already sticky, and his sweat smothered the light scent of his cologne. He was the bug caught against a summer screen. His attempt at projecting boredom didn't work. He looked down at his hands and pressed both flat on the table to stop them shaking. If he saw his hands, she did too. He tried to steady himself. "Detective, I've given that story at least ten times. This is, excuse me, a waste of time."

"We don't think so. Let's begin, shall we." The grim cat and mouse chase was on.

Connor pulled both hands closer as a small defense. "My class ended earlier than usual. I drove straight home. When I walked through the front door, I saw nothing that stood out. I was halfway up the stairs when I realized the house was completely dark. That, and my mother didn't call out, 'You're home.' I turned and came back down the stairs. I flipped on the hall lights." Connor ran his fist across his mouth. "That's when I saw Dad's leg."

Damiano interrupted Tibbett's recounting with a blunt question.

"On the Tuesday night, or Wednesday, before the deaths, what was your reaction to learning that your father intended to disinherit you?"

Connor leaped up and nearly knocked the table on its side. He steadied it without a word. "Can't you at least be civil to me?"

Damiano didn't hesitate. "Sit down, sir, or I'll have you handcuffed to the chair."

Connor pushed his chair loudly into place and sat down on it hard.

"We didn't invite you to tea, Mr. Tibbett. This is an interrogation, and you are a prime suspect. Now, answer the question truthfully. As I've advised you, your words can be used against you in court. We know that two days after you found out about the will, both parents were dead."

"I didn't request a lawyer ten years ago because I didn't murder my parents. Nothing has changed. I have come here today in good faith."

"Your parents are still dead, and you found them."

"Finding them is not a crime."

"Let's get back to my original question. Did your father inform you he intended to disinherit you?"

CHAPTER SIXTY

"MY FATHER TOLD ME on Tuesday night." Connor's face twitched, but all he offered up was a thin smile. He moved back against the chair.

Damiano hoped to explore and target that discovery, so she was undeterred by Tibbett's reaction. "Detective Matte and I don't believe in coincidence. Learning you were about to be disinherited, and two days later, we learn that both your parents are dead strengthens our investigation. To us coincidence is just something previously unknown brought to light."

Connor reached into the inside pocket of his blazer, extracted an envelope and handed it to Damiano. "Though I received the money, within two weeks, I set up a trust fund for my three nephews. Is that a point for me?"

Between her teeth, Damiano said, "It is. That's quite commendable as well. Let's continue."

"That night, I told my father I never expected anything from him, and left the room while he was explaining how Emma and her children needed the help. I had confidence I could make money. It wasn't a concern then and it still isn't." *Is that all they have learned? Maybe I won't have to…*

Connor never had the chance to finish his thought.

"Our biggest stumbling block has been the absence of the weapon. We know the make, the GSR, the gunshot residue, such a weapon leaves behind, but without the actual weapon, we couldn't close the case. So, let's go back to where you saw your father's leg."

Damiano could not believe the sudden change in Tibbett. His face blanched, his eyes watered in fear, and a wicked jolt shook him as though he been struck in the stomach.

"I don't think the trauma caught me immediately. I ran to my father, with two fingers I felt for a pulse. All I felt was my own. I stepped back into quicksand. I couldn't move, I felt I was choking, I never took my eyes off my dad. It felt like we were caught in some horrid tableau. Then I saw frothy blood bubble from my father's nostrils. He…"

Damiano cut in, "We know you took the weapon – we know you hid it in the car."

Connor wasn't listening or couldn't. "He opened his bloody eye. He looked straight at me. Then, down at the gun, and back at me. He wanted me to protect him and my mom from the scandal and gossip. All my life I thought of what my father never gave me. I never figured he might need something from me. I grabbed a glove beside the car keys on the table by the front door, and took hold of the gun. It lay on the sofa near my father's thigh. I ran outside and slid the glove and gun under the front seat. When I ran back into the house, it was as though I hadn't moved. I stared at my father for some recognition, but he was dead. How long I stood there I can't say. I finally called 911. I didn't recognize my own voice, forgot my address, couldn't name my street, and ended up shouting 'Help! I need help!'"

"Connor Tibbett, I am arresting you for obstruction of justice. You've wasted years of valuable time for three Major Crime investigations by deliberately obstructing justice and contaminating the crime scene."

"No, not willfully. Don't you see, my father needed me. I did something right. I helped my father."

"You'll be held here overnight and…"

"Listen to me. Let me finish, please. You see, when I came back into the house, there was no blood on my father's upper lip. It may never have been there. He may not have killed my mother. There is a chance I was wrong. Wrong about everything!" Connor was weeping and imploring Damiano to hear him, to listen. "Can't you understand? I wasn't trying to break any laws. I was trying to help my father." Connor prayed that Damiano would have the acuity to understand what he was saying. His face flushed; his nostrils flared. "I'd looked around. There were no footprints on the carpet, but still… Can't you see? I had to help my father. It wasn't a choice. It wasn't a choice." He whispered the last words.

For the first time, Damiano subdued the undercurrent of her contempt and referred to Tibbett by his first name. "Connor, listen to me. What did you do with gun?"

"That Thursday night, I threw it into Lac-St-Louis to spare my father the shame of a murder/suicide. He couldn't help himself. Can't you see I had to do something? He needed *me* for once!"

"You idiot! There might have been prints on that weapon. We could have traced the weapon and run the prints. Solved the case!"

Matte was already leaving the monitoring room when Damiano shouted, "Pierre, get in here!"

EPILOGUE

Detective Matte had been listening and observing Tibbett's body language.

"Wait here and don't move," Damiano left the room and to meet Matte. "Wasted, the whole two weeks!"

"Calm down. He couldn't hear you; he was so intent on his own story. We got further than any team. Did you actually hear what he said?"

"Pure stupidity. All of it!"

"No. He was emotionally compromised," Pierre calmly corrected Damiano. "Try to see the whole picture, Toni."

Damiano was furious. "Ninety-nine percent, murder/suicide, and one percent dangling, lost in the muddy waters of Lac-St-Louis."

"The weapon was leaning against his father's thigh, with GSR residue on his fingers. It's as close to a solve as we are going to get. Sometimes, close has to be enough."

"What will the chief say?"

"We know that Donat has had unsolved cases in his history, I've checked. He survived and went on to become chief. We have to proceed with Tibbett."

Damiano opened the door. Her hard stare was icy. Matte's face softened. Tibbett struggled to his feet, devastated. "What now?" he asked.

"Book him," she told Matte.

"I need my one phone call." Matte handed him his phone while Damiano glared. "Tim, you have the number for Raymond Daoust. Against his advice, I told the truth, but he knows what to do now. Thanks for your support."

Matte took his phone and opened a door in the back of the interrogation room that led directly to a cell. Matte put a hand on Tibbett's shoulder and ushered him inside. "It won't be long before an officer performs the booking, prints and photo."

Connor paced, wondering if there was any value to the truth. He didn't notice the size of the cell, or the other suspect, three cells down, who had noticed him. The simple cot looked good to him, and he lay down with both arms behind his head. *The truth will set you free.* Ha! He was locked in a cell. He felt a hysterical laugh surfacing and swallowed it. Raymond Daoust had to find a way to save his livelihood. Obstruction was a felony. He couldn't work in finance with a felony. Sweat puddled under his arms and trickled across his stomach. His eyes welled up and he swiped the tears away. *I thought taking the gun was between you and me. But, it's not. They found out. Dad, you have to help me now!*

The booking, the prints, the photo, the loss of clothes was one big swipe. Connor wondered if a woman who'd been abused felt the same way, cut down until identity was lost in separate pieces until you ceased to exist. Connor sat alone scared. The twin burdens of responsibility and guilt released him. Connor didn't understand how he just lay down on the cot and fell asleep, with no dreams.

Chief Donat listened to his senior detectives summarize their findings. Unexpectedly, he made both Damiano and Matte smile. "Criminals we know, make mistakes we can predict and understand. Amateurs don't know what the hell they're doing, and leave us punching air. As you've said, Tibbett didn't gain anything, was emotionally disturbed, and trying to help his father. At his age, under the same conditions, I might have done the same thing."

To Damiano's astonishment, Matte, whom she knew had suffered from his father's hateful bias, agreed. "You men!"

"Murder/suicide is what we'll give the press release. In small print – with reservation. It is common that when a male commits suicide, he takes his wife with him. Your notes stated that there was shock on the wife's face. Unfortunately, that's all we have. We're suspending our investigation. Detective Damiano, calm yourself. We can't find the gun and there'd be no prints on it now even if we did. We gave this case three attempts. Reality is a tough chew."

Connor Tibbett's case went to arbitration. Connor's lawyer, Raymond Daoust—an Atticus Finch—was a deceptive, wise and gentle man who argued deftly: "On the night of the tragedy, Connor Tibbett, 22, was an emotionally disturbed young man, scarcely aware of his actions. He wasn't sure he had even taken the weapon, couldn't speak, or recall the name of his street. He retched and almost fainted. His only rational thought was to spare his dad and mother further humiliation. He even imagined his father was asking for his help. The young man had no priors, and did not gain from his action. There was clearly never any intent to subvert justice. This was a young man traumatized by the brutal death of both parents.

"He cannot work at his livelihood with a felony charge. I beg the court for leniency, for compassion." He argued for a suspended sentence and a good deal of community service. The wait was on.

While Connor was free on bail, the insurance company sought to have their money, six hundred thousand dollars, with accrued interest, recouped. Connor was no amateur where money was concerned. He pointed out that the case was suspended, not closed. Under his expertise, the trust fund had doubled. He offered to reimburse three hundred and fifty thousand with the proviso that they agreed to close the Tibbett file. They replied within a week that his offer was accepted with its condition. Connor continued to work and wait for the decision on his own case. The courts, he knew, were backlogged. He was forced to learn patience.

To his surprise, some time before the verdict, he sensed a soul-searching pride he hadn't felt since his youth. He had finally done right by his father. The joy was almost physical, but fleeting. His parents were dead and they took with them the reasons, the anger, the love and all hope of change. Their deaths were the brutal reality he'd blocked for ten years. And now what remained was only the memory of that Thursday night, the sadness of their awful embrace, and the arears of love. For a moment, he couldn't move, he couldn't breathe. *I forgive you.* Were these words Connor's pardon or his father's blessing? Connor didn't know.

When Connor and Timothy had their first quiet time, Connor was adamant. "If I end up with any prison time, I want you to bail on me. Start a new life. I can't bear that I would be ruining your life as well as my own."

"I hope one day, you'll learn what love is. I'm here for the duration because I love you. Whatever happens, we'll work it out together." Timothy saw Connor's astonishment. "There's no need to say anything."

"I will anyway. So, you're my shining knight."

"I like that."

Martin Heron read the *Gazette* with special interest. "With reservation" rebooted his avid interest. "I knew it! Should I call the authorities?" Martin broke a strict edict of not drinking before dinner. He drank two glasses of wine at ten-thirty in the morning. "Bravo for me! I could solve their case. I, Martin Heron." The only thing more important to Martin than fame was mortification. "Hughes has proof I was stalking her. I look like a fool in that video. The Ogilvy's manager will tell the police I'm paranoid. They will dismiss me as a nutcase. I have a law degree, for God's sake! But the fact is, I don't even know the Tibbetts or care about them." He had more wine. "Full of sound and fury – that's Martin." He simply fell asleep and spilled red wine on his cream Queen Anne wing chair.

Damiano was despondent. Matte wasn't happy either. "We have our first unsolved. We are too good to fail. God dammit!"

"You have a better win than a solved case. You have a second chance. You beat the cancer scare."

Damiano's shoulders slackened, and she smiled broadly, "I did, didn't I."

Sandra Hughes had read the paper with studied care to the Tibbett article. Carefully folding the *Gazette,* she left it aside. Carrying an antique wooden chair to the door of the apartment, Sandra stood on it. She lifted a brass crucifix off its clip and carried it to the kitchen. After polishing the cross, she brought it to the bedroom. There, she laid it under the spare pillow beside her own. "You can rest easy now James." She walked over to her closet and found the two identical letters. She stood reading each, pinching her eyes with sad recollection of the chaos and grief one page had wreaked on their lives. Sandra folded them and gave both one final look. The only break in Hughes's demeanor was a delicious smile, smeared with tears, as she tore the letters into little pieces. She cupped the pieces in both hands, squeezing them as she tossed them into her recycling bag. Sandra did not look back as she left the room.

ACKNOWLEDGEMENTS

The complex father-son relationship was of interest to me in the writing of this book. A reluctance to cede dominance marks the timeless Greek myths from the Titans, the elder gods, to the twelve Olympians. Destruction of offspring illustrates a need to preserve power from their progeny. At a turning point, sons strike back to wrench control--some with vengeance, some with pity.

Sacrifice is the principle of biblical relationships. God the Father and Son, Abraham and Isaac. Generally, the sacrifice is for good, nevertheless it is a test of fealty too. In Shakespeare's *Hamlet*, the son is the avenger of his father's death. In Faulkner's *The Sound and the Fury*, Quentin Compson, well-educated, does not resolve his parental and social dilemmas and takes his own life. Generally, the patriarch is a guide, a leader and a teacher, but with flawed humans, there is always corruption.

I recall a therapist's lecture. "It's not uncommon for some parents not to feel love for their child. Ironically, despite this, children love their parents and are forgiving." In this novel, Connor Tibbett is an interesting study.

A shoutout to St. Mary's Hospital for their assistance, their enthusiastic approach to their work and the cleanliness of the hospital. The Montreal General Hospital reminds me of Grand Central Station. There are no amateurs here. It's a beehive of busy people whose information is precise and quickly given. Here, one feels safe.

I have a wonderful team for signings: What began as the 'great duo': Gina Pingitore and Cynthia Iorio, who even travelled to Ontario, has grown. Linda Morand, Liz MacRae and Robert Idsinga joined us and added additional success. All are generous and marvelous at sales. Once more, I am grateful for the unwavering generous support of Kathy Panet, Claire Coleman, Noreen Barrett, Hamid and Maryam Afshari, and the Kindellans: Maureen, Frank, Mary, Kevin and Stephen, and Steve & Helga Lawrence. Dick Irvin's check-in calls keep me on my toes. Thanks to Dorothy Puga for your good work and effort with the author's photo. Gratitude aplenty to Sonali Karnick for her wonderful support through the years.

Gina Pingitore and Margaret Goldik, are integral partners— astute readers and editors—they have travelled the whole journey. Exceptional women and dearest friends. I count myself blessed. To my editor, Simon Dardick, I owe joy in my life. It is my good fortune to be his friend.